Flawed

By

Shior la queen

Flawed
Copyright © 2019 by Shior la queen. All rights reserved.

No part of this publication may be reproduced, stored in a retrieval system or transmitted in any way by any means, electronic, mechanical, photocopy, recording or otherwise without the prior permission of the author except as provided by USA copyright law.

Scripture quotations, unless otherwise indicated, are taken from the *Holy Bible, King James Version*, Cambridge, 1769. Used by permission. All rights reserved. The opinions expressed by the author are not necessarily those of Fountain of Life Publisher's House.

Published by Fountain of Life Publisher's House P. O. Box 922612 Norcross, GA 30010
Please Email Manuscripts to: publish@pariceparker.biz
www.pariceparker.biz

Fountain of Life Publisher's House is committed to excellence in the publishing industry. The Company reflects the philosophy established by the founder, based on Psalm 68:11, "The Lord gave the word and great was the company of those who published it."

Book design copyright © 2019 by Leon Bull & Parice C Parker
All rights reserved.
Authored by Shior la queen
Editor: Nichol Burris

Published in the United States of America

ISBN: 9781092521468

4.2.2019

Table of Contents

Introduction
Dedication

	Page
Chapter One	
Peaches October 1999 "Sugar Shit"	07
Chapter Two	
The Mishap	42
Chapter Three	
Screw Up	47
Chapter Four	
Loyalty & Lies	56
Chapter Five	
Love Triangle	72
Chapter Six	
Monster In Disguise	87
Chapter Seven	
Incredible	98
Chapter Eight	
Wacko	103
Chapter Nine	
Til Death Do Us Part	125

Introduction

Peaches were born and raised in da dirty south of Georgia, East Point to be exact. A beautiful, humble soul with an incredible imagination. She was once lost in the fire from fuck-ups to mistakes and regrets that left her homeless, overlooked, and abandoned. Being she was now 36 yrs full of pride with a heart of gold from puppy love, to betrayal, deception, and revenge that led to success. Peaches, now realize her gift was discovered summer of "1992."

Shior la queen

Deditcation

To the Summer of "1992."

Shior la queen

Chapter 1

Peaches October 1999 "Sugar to Shit"

Once Peaches laid eyes on Rell it was like love at first sight. He was so handsome as he walked up and grabbed Peaches around her waist. She pushed him away trying to act shy, knowing she liked his aggressiveness. "Excuse me!" she replied, "do I know you?" Rell responded, "Imma make you my baby momma and walked off." Peaches rolled her eyes and continued to enjoy the talent show she was attending at Columbia High School with her cousin, Megan. OMG!!! Peaches tugged Megan's arm, "Gurl, Zay here." "Where?" replied Megan (Breaking her neck trying to look, knowing his cousin East was with him.)

Standing out, Peaches and Megan were dressed to impress. They both had on a fresh pair of all white

Air Forces. Peaches had on a pair of tan fitted khaki pants with a tan tank top with the khaki jacket to match. Megan was on the same accord, but she wore blue jeans with the matching jacket. East and Zay were both fine as hell. Peaches met Zay at Sparkles, the skating rink in Riverdale, and he was her first love. When he moved to Decatur they lost contact and Peaches' heart had been broken ever since. When Zay and Peaches' eyes met, they were both smiling from ear to ear, and East had the biggest crush on Megan. She was pretty too, standing at about 5'2 with hazel brown eyes, a slim waist, and cute in the face. When they approached each other, everyone hugged, exchanged numbers, and departed. As Peaches and Megan were exiting the restroom, heading back to their seats, they saw Rell waiting patiently with his phone number in his hand; hoping Peaches wouldn't turn him down. She took it and kept walking, not wanting to show that she was happy as hell on the inside. When the show was over, Peaches talked Megan's ear off the whole way home about how fine Zay was.

Peaches lived on the East Side of Atlanta and attended Southwest Dekalb High School; she was a junior and ready to graduate. Peaches had just transferred from Riverdale which was on the south side of Atlanta because her parents had recently divorced, meaning she really didn't have any friends. Megan was the only friend she needed; they were first cousins and got along well.

The next day, it was Peaches' first day of school, and boy, was she nervous. The school was huge, and she had never seen that many black people; it was scary. In her old school, the diversity level was through the roof: blacks, whites, Mexicans, and more. This was much different, and she had no choice but to get used to it. When Peaches got home from school, she decided to give Rell a call. He had been on her mind all day. As she began to dial his number, her sister walked in her room being extra loud and rude, causing Peaches to scream at the top of her lungs, "LEAH GET OUT!" She rolled her eyes and slammed the door, knowing Peaches would make her cry for being a smart ass. Peaches thought maybe that was a sign not to call. She wasn't dating anyone at the time, but she had a lot of Niggas waiting in line for a chance.

Peaches was sexy, dark skinned, and had gray eyes. Her shape was out of this world: a flat stomach with thick thighs and thick black hair. She had a piercing in her nose and a swag you couldn't resist. Her phone rang. "Hello!" she answered. "What's up boo?" he said. It was her homeboy, Cap, a dope boy from Chandler Road that moved heavy weight. Only 2 years older than Peaches, he was head over heels for her. He liked Peaches because she was different from most girls he dealt with. She was a good girl and not a thot like what he was used to. He was street smart while she was book smart. That was why he liked her so much. "Wasup, Cap?" She responded. "When can I see you? I miss looking into those beautiful eyes of yours." Peaches wasn't really looking for anything serious with anyone at the time. In a daze, she forgot she was on the phone with Cap. "Peaches! Damn, why you so quiet, Ma?" he said. "No reason. I'm about to start on my homework, give me twenty minutes," Peaches replied, "I'll call you back." "Cool!" Cap said. Right after, Peaches grabbed Rell's number and finally called, "Hello, may I speak to Rell?" His homeboy he lived with told her to hold on. It took a while before he came to the phone. "Hello! Hey, wassup?" he said, "Who is this?" "It's me, Peaches, from the talent show." He responded, "Oooh, you finally decided to call huh?" Peaches giggled and began to blush. They talked for hours, like they had known each other for years. Rell was a dope boy too, so school wasn't in his vocabulary. He understood Peaches had to get some rest and he respected that, so they ended the call with a goodnight. Peaches then closed her eyes wishing she was sleeping right next to (Zay).

The next day by third period, Peaches started to dose off. She was hoping Mrs. Rountree would shut the hell up. She hated the fact that she didn't get any sleep the night before. As soon as 3:15 hit, the bell rung and Peaches up and left. As usual, the halls were packed. When Peaches got to her locker she felt someone tap her shoulder. She couldn't believe her eyes. "What the hell u doing here boy?" Rell smiling, "I came to pick you up and take you home," he responded. "Aww, how sweet!" Rell began to grab some of Peaches' books and took her to the car. He even opened the door for her to get in. Once Rell drove off, he asked Peaches if she was hungry. When she responded, "Yes," he stopped at McDonald's and bought Peaches something to eat. Afterwards, he took her home. Before Peaches got out the car, she noticed a hair bow on the floor that looked like it belonged to a woman, but she didn't say anything. Rell walked Peaches to the door where she then thanked him for the ride and gave him a hug before he left. After making it in the house, she ran to her bed, jumped in it, and dosed off. It was about 8:30pm when she woke up from her nap. She went through her caller ID to see if she had any missed calls, when her phone rang. "Hello!" she said. "Wassup, Baby?" he replied. It was Rell. "Hey Boo! What you doing?" she said in her best flirty voice. Thinking about you," Rell replied. Peaches just couldn't resist, "Whose car are you driving?" she asked anxiously. Rell laughed and replied, "Ohh, that's my sister's car." "Mmhmm," Peaches replied (with skepticism). In the back of her mind, she knew he was lying. Peaches' other line beeped. "Hold on punk," she said. It was Megan, "Wassup, Bitch?" "Hold on, let me get Rell off the other line," she replied. When Peaches returned to Megan, she told her how Rell popped up at her school and the bow she saw in the car. Megan explained to Peaches about when she talked to East he had invited them to a bar-b-que that weekend. They knew they had to be on point. Peaches couldn't wait because she was ready to see Zay. The last encounter they had was at her house before she moved to Decatur when her mom was at work.

Peaches and Megan snuck Zay and East in the house, being rebellious, knowing damn well if they got caught their funeral was gonna be held the very next day. Peaches was only twelve at the time she lied and told Zay she was thirteen he was fourteen. Peaches was so mature for her age, plus, back then you really couldn't even tell. Zay kissed Peaches all through the night. She was on cloud nine and didn't even think of coming back down. That Saturday evening, Megan was at Peaches' house early "Peaches!" Megan called, "get up, lets go to the mall." Annie, Peaches' mom, came in the room and gave them both a kiss before she ventured off to work (as usual). Peaches' mom was a writer for Ebony Magazine. Annie always worked hard so her kids wouldn't have to want for anything. "Peaches and her sister was always hip to the latest fashion, and the hottest blogs before anybody else. I want the kitchen cleaned before you leave here," Annie proclaimed. Halfway awake, Peaches replied with a faint, "Yes ma'am."

Post coming from nearly every shop in the mall, Peaches and Megan returned home and got dressed. Peaches put on her Nike Air Max, a Rock-a--Wear outfit, a gold Rolex, and a gold herringbone. Megan bought pink All Star Chuck Taylors, a pink tennis skirt to match, a white tank top, and a pink head band. After arriving at the park, it wasn't long before they noticed how packed it was with Niggas. Bitches were twerking on top of cars, music blasting, and barbecue smoke lit the air. It was like Freaknik in '96. Peaches and Megan went to sit on the car. Not long after they got out to get a better view of who all was there, Peaches pulled out her 3.5 and began rolling. Of course, she was getting ready to smoke her Mary Jane.

While chillin' and enjoying the scene, they realized they were listening to *Off Glass by Trina*. That's when they witnessed Zay pull up in a 1980 Cutlass Supreme with 15'inch rims, all black, with white interior and was clean as hell. Seeing him get out of the car, Peaches literally choked off the blunt. She saw Cap hop out of the backseat. "What the Fuck!!! How do they know each other?" She almost pissed on herself.

As soon as Zay had seen her, Megan walked off to go speak to East. Cap was still tagging along behind Zay walking towards Peaches. "Oh shit!"was her only thought. Staggering, trying to find the right words, Zay approached and hugged her tight, so he could kiss her on the cheek. Cap abruptly intervened saying "Aye, man, y'all know each other?" Zay responded with something jaw dropping to Cap, "I want you to meet Peaches, my first love," If looks could kill, Cap just killed Peaches in cold blood. Cap walked off without saying a word. She knew exactly what that meant, leaving her with too many self-conflicting thoughts. Zay told Peaches to enjoy herself and he would be back to check on her. The only thing that could make Peaches feel better was another blunt to ease her mind.

Megan walked back over to Peaches in total shock, even she didn't know what to say. Megan looked at Peaches insinuating the obvious (what the hell is goin' on, Bitch)? She had so many questions for Peaches. "What just happened? What did I miss?" While Peaches was explaining to Megan what just happened, Rell walked by, but didn't see Peaches. That's when Megan looked at Peaches and said, "Bitch, it's time to go." This was just too much for Peaches. It appeared as though everyone knew each other: Rell, Zay, and Cap were all from the same hood and digging the same girl. Peaches saw that Cap, Zay, and Rell were having an intriguing discussion with each other. Peaches was now positive that it was time to go. When Zay came back, Peaches was gone. He pulled out his cellphone, called Peaches, and said, "Hello, Bae where you at?" Peaches lied and said she wasn't feeling good so she left. Zay told her if she felt any better to come back so they could at least spend some quality time together. Peaches liked how that sounded, but she just couldn't go back.

Both Megan and Peaches decided to stay in and make it a girl's night. They put on pajamas, ordered pizza, popped popcorn, and made ice cream sundaes; hell, Leah even joined them. The girls stayed up all night talking about what had happened that day.

Weeks later, it was December 23rd and Peaches' mom was still wrapping gifts and getting dinner prepared for Christmas Day. Peaches fell back since the day of the bar-b-que. She hadn't talked to Cap, Rell, or Zay. That night was the first night Megan and Peaches decided to step out. They went to Scores, the sports bar on Wesley Chapel Rd. While entering, Peaches spotted Zay. It felt like heaven again. Of course, that's every time she sees him. She then ran to Zay and hugged him, not even caring if anyone was there with him. He had a lot of women flocking at his feet. While hugging, Peaches whispered into Zay's ear, "Happy belated birthday!" Zay smiled, his birthday was November 3rd. He then said, "You really do love me huh?" Peaches smiled and replied with, "Yes!" They enjoyed each other's company the entire night. That next day was Christmas Eve, Peaches, Leah, and their mom went to the mall to pick up a couple more gifts. That's when Peaches spotted Zay. They exchanged smiles and hugged. Peaches introduced Zay to her mom and told her how Zay was her first love. Annie responded with a pleasant, "Hello!" Peaches was blushing; she loved her some Zay. Before they walked off, Zay turned around, put his hand up to his ear, and mouthed to Peaches, "Call me." Peaches replied with, "Ok!" and departed. For some reason, when Peaches got home, she couldn't stop thinking about Zay. She called him that next day but got no answer. Later on that night Peaches' phone rang. She answered with a disinterested "Hello!" It was Cap, he greeted and went right into the gossip, "P, did you hear what happened?" Peaches answered, "No what?" "Zay just got killed," exclaimed Cap. Megan and Peaches arrived at Donald Trimble Funeral home on 2nd Ave. The police had to patrol traffic because there were so many people. Cars drove bumper to bumper all the way down to Glennwood Rd. After driving around in continuous circles, Megan finally found a place to park; Peaches sat in the car, still in total shock. She found herself wanting to wake up from a bad dream and wishing this wasn't real. "Peaches, you ok?" Megan asked. She didn't answer, she just nodded her head. When Peaches finally got out of the car, she noticed people were everywhere. It was packed to capacity. Before you even got a chance to step in the doors, there was loud crying. Megan held Peaches' hand because she knew this was very hard for her and Megan intended to help Peaches through this. The line to view Zay's body extended outside of the doors. Peaches and Megan stood in line for at least two hours. When the line finally began to move, Peaches used every ounce of strength and courage to walk closer. She had to hold on to each pew for balance with one hand while Megan held the other. Getting closer to the casket, Peaches felt like she was going to faint. She started to get hot flashes and began to cry heavily. She couldn't hold it any longer.

That's when it had hit her, the love of her life was gone. The screams and yelling were something that Peaches couldn't stomach. Megan saw Peaches gather up the rest of her strength and walk up to Zay's casket. She put her hand on it and began to cry. She told Zay that she loved him and that she was gonna miss him. This was one of the hardest days for Peaches. One that she would carry around for what she believed to be the rest of her now, miserable life.

Finally, she got to the casket. She just couldn't bear to look at Zay. It was so painful to see him like that. Peaches ran out. After running after Peaches, Megan found herself crying. This was weighing down the both of them. The gravesite was packed just like the bar-b-que East had invited them to. Zay was loved by everyone. Everyone who was any relation to Zay knew that whoever murdered him, had to be a hater. The story that was going around was that he was minding his own business while driving his black escalade with "22"inch rims when someone jumped in his car and shot him in the back of his head. Gasping for breath, Zay ran into a tree and was left to die. Two weeks later, Peaches' phone rang, "Hello!" she answered. It was Cap, "Hey P! What you doing?" "Nothing, just sitting here watching TV, wassup?" she replied. Cap responded, "I was calling to see if you wanted to go see Zay. We could stop and get some flowers if you want." Peaches answered with a semi-shocked, "Sure, I would love that, Cap." In her mind, she really didn't know what to think. The last time Peaches and Cap had spoken was at the barbecue when he walked away furious at her for not telling him about Zay. He picked Peaches up and stopped at the nearest florist shop. After getting to the gravesite, Peaches felt the sadness coming on again. It was cold, so Cap put his arm around Peaches. As they both stood there lost for words, Cap went through the past times of his good friend as he poured a bottle of Henny on his homeboy's grave saying,"This is for you." As for Peaches, she still couldn't bring herself to the simple fact that Zay was never coming back.

Four months later, it was April of the year 2000. As soon as Peaches walked in her house, she heard the phone ringing from downstairs. After she made it upstairs to her room in no rush, it was too late. She scrolled through her caller ID and noticed a number she didn't recognize. After calling it back, a female answered, "Hello!" "Yes, I'm returning a call, this is Peaches." she said. The female replied, "Yeah, this is Tawana, Rell's girlfriend. I found this number in his phone." Peaches laughed and replied, "Ok, how can I help you?" Tawana told Peaches Rell was in jail, and when he got out she was not letting him come back. She went on to say that he had been cheating on her and how the whole thing came about. They chatted for a few; Peaches listened to what Tawana had to say and told her to tell Rell to call her when she spoke with him. After hanging up, Peaches' came to a realization; last year, her woman's intuition told her that something wasn't right about the car. Rell's "sister's car" was, in fact, his girlfriend's, and he had a lot of explaining to do. Two days later, Peaches came home from school to find out that Rell sent a message through her mom to tell her he was sorry for what happened. Tawana told Rell that she had spoken to Peaches and he was pissed. He knew Peaches wouldn't speak to him again. Rell knew then that he fucked up. All he had to do was keep it real with Peaches. A year later, Peaches was finally a senior and was able to pay her school dues because she got a job working at Ingles Supermarket after school. Peaches hadn't decided yet to what college to attend. She was just riding the wave and enjoying her senior year. At that time, she was also still enjoying the single life. Out of the blue, Peaches received a call from Rell, "Yo!" Peaches answered, not knowing who it was. "What you want," Peaches asked. Rell responded, "I'm sorry for not being honest and I know I messed up, but I want to make it up by taking you to the prom." The prom was two months away and Peaches didn't have a date yet, but instead of agreeing, she told Rell she'd think about. Peaches didn't want any more drama, so she asked what happened to Tawana. Rell told her he lives with his sister and that he would never lie to her again. Peaches wasn't sure what to believe, she told Rell that she would call him back later. That night, Peaches and Megan decided to go out. They went to Club Bounce, it was the new hotspot, right off of Bankhead Hwy. Megan and Peaches both wore daisy dukes, a crop top, and the new Air Jordan 6+ "Olympic," they were matching from head to toe. The moment they got in the club, Peaches was on the dance floor; she hadn't been out in a while, so this was well needed. A tall, dark-skinned guy started dancing with Peaches. As close as they were, it appeared as if they had come to the club together. With the way he was against Peaches, anyone would of thought they were dating. He asked Peaches her name and if he could have her number. He was a cutie, so she didn't mind. Afterwards, Peaches went to go find Megan to show her who the guy was. Megan responded, "Oh that's Shaheed. I know him from school." Megan attended Clark Atlanta University in Atlanta, GA. Megan told Peaches that her friend, Kee-Kee, who also attended the school was seeing him. Peaches should have known. It was only a matter of time for the truth to be revealed. Later in the year, she met another guy, Chris, at a party. He liked Peaches so much that he gave her a ride home from work every night. Chris was up front about his off and on relationship with his girlfriend, and Peaches was ok with that. Chris wasn't even her type, besides, Zay still held a piece of her heart. Peaches finally decided that she would attend Advance Career Training after graduation: she would take a trade only for a year. Annie surprised Peaches by passing down her 2000 Rodeo Jeep so she could have reliable transportation. Peaches was excited; she was able to go as she pleased without having to hitch a ride. The only condition with the car was that Peaches had to promise her mom that she would maintain good grades. Two months later, Peaches and Shaheed were dating. They were looking forward to going to prom together. Tonight was the night; they wore gold and ivory to match. Peaches had on a stunning gold long gown with the back out that fitted perfect to her shape. Shaheed wore an ivory tuxedo with a gold vest and along with all white gators. Peaches was surprised to see Shaheed arrive in a "1960" old school convertible, all white with the top down. It was fully equipped with TV's and "24" inch rims.

Peaches was speechless. Shaheed was going to make sure this was going to be a night Peaches would remember forever. After Annie took pictures, Shaheed and Peaches rode through the city with the top back, enjoying the breeze. Peaches sat in the middle next to Shaheed while he drove with one hand on the steering wheel and his other around Peaches. As they were riding, people were blowing their horns and waving at them. They looked so cute. The night was going to be spectacular. Shaheed took Peaches to Houston's for dinner before prom. Later, they arrived at the Marriott hotel. Shaheed got valet parking. He got out the car and opened Peaches' door. He grabbed her hand as they strutted down the red carpet looking like bags of money. The moment they walked, they went to take pictures. Peaches and Shaheed made sure they remained on the dance floor all night. He videotaped every move Peaches made, and she loved every bit of it. "Make it Last Forever" by Keith Sweat began playing. Shaheed asked, "Peaches, may I have this dance?" She smiled and said, "Sure." They swayed back and forth as they held each other tight. He whispered in Peaches' ear, "You look so good baby." Peaches replied with a thank you and gave Shaheed a kiss that he wouldn't forget. As soon as prom ended, they cruised the town with the lights on in the car. It was the like the scene found in the movie "Grease." It was about 2:25am when Shaheed asked Peaches if she was ready to go home. She told him "Yes!" He told himself he wasn't gonna ask for any pussy that night, but he did want it and badly. Peaches looked so good he was excited just being next to her. The moment they arrived at Peaches' house, Shaheed walked her to the door. Then they shared a sensational hug and kiss. Peaches thanked him for everything; he told her she deserved it and that he would do anything to make her happy. "I will call you once I make it home," Shaheed said, "so make sure you stay up until I call." Peaches replied, "OK." Peaches made it to her room where Megan was there waiting to hear every detail about how the night went. They stayed up all night talking until Shaheed called. Three weeks later, it was May 24th: Graduation Day. Peaches graduated with a 4.0, and she was happy as hell that high school was over. Shaheed was there with a dozen roses. He told Peaches he was proud of her and wanted to take her out that night to celebrate.

Graduation went smoothly, and Peaches' family was waiting for her at the house. They prepared a feast with all her favorite foods: Collards, Mac n Cheese, Deviled Eggs, Dressing, Ribs, Potato Salad, Crab Legs, Shrimp, and much more. For dessert, they had Sweet Potato Pie, Key Lime Pie, Strawberry Shortcake, and Banana Pudding.

When dinner was over, Peaches thanked everyone for coming. She received over 500 dollars from various family members. She knew she was really about to have a ball that night. But first, she had to help her mom clean the kitchen.

Peaches and Megan decided to hit the local club, "Bounce" since it was always lit. Shaheed told her he would meet them there. Upon arriving, they saw it was packed more than usual. Peaches was afraid she wasn't going to be able to find Shaheed. The club was so crowded that the Marshals were called and no one else was permitted to enter the club. When Peaches finally found a place to sit, she rolled up. That's when she spotted Shaheed shooting pool (that was his hobby). Megan dipped off into the crowd leaving Peaches by herself, but she didn't mind. Megan knew that as long as Peaches had some weed, she was fine. Moments later, Shaheed noticed Peaches sitting there watching him. She blew him a kiss; he smiled and winked back at her.

He sent a waitress over to her so she could order whatever she wanted.

After he finished playing pool, he walked over to Peaches and asked if she wanted to take some pictures. Out of boredom, she replied, "Yes!" By then, Peaches was on her 4th blunt, 3rd drink, and was now ordering some wings to get rid of her post high munchies. She was higher than a kite. Meanwhile, Megan was chatting with a few friends she went to school with. From time to time, she made sure to keep Peaches in her sight. Shaheed told Peaches he was ready to go, and she told him to meet her at her house.

When Peaches and Megan left the club, Shaheed was at the house waiting, just as he promised. Her plan was to let him spend the night since her mom had to work late. Shaheed and Peaches fucked all night long until it was time for him to leave. He got up, making sure not to wake Peaches. He got dressed, kissed Peaches on the forehead, and headed home. One year later, on October 15th, Peaches graduated with a Medical Assistant Diploma. Shaheed came to support his "baby" at her graduation. After getting home, he surprised her with a water fall portrait that lit up. She could even hear the water falling. Peaches loved it and him. Months later, it was December 25th, Christmas Day and Shaheed's family invited Peaches over for dinner. She was nervous because she had never met his parents before; this was going to be interesting. This day was bitter sweet for Peaches; her heart still ached at the thought of Zay. Every time she thought of him she'd whisper, "I Love You!" When they arrived at Shaheed's house, his dad said, "Whoa! Where did you get this beauty from?" Shaheed laughed and introduced Peaches to his family. He showed Peaches to his room, so she could put her belongings away. Later in the day, they ate dinner. They laughed and talked, his family really wanted to get to know Peaches. After dinner, she helped Miss Roxanne, his mom, clean the kitchen. When it was time for bed, Peaches slept in Shaheed's room while Shaheed slept on the couch. No matter how horny they both were, they had no choice but to sleep apart and in different parts of the house. Peaches was mad as hell. She wanted some dick so bad that night. They both decided to wait until he took Peaches home that next day. Three weeks had past and Peaches noticed something different about Shaheed; he was acting distant lately. When she called him, he was never home. She was trying to contact him about the good news she had about getting her own place. Now, they could spend more time together and not have to worry about their parents; this was the privacy they had always wanted. Peaches' phone rang, "House of cutie this is beauty," she answered. Shaheed laughed, "What's up Stanky?" he replied. "Stanky" was the nickname Shaheed had given her a while back. She answered, "Nigga, don't 'wassup' me! Where the fuck you been?" Shaheed tried to tell her that he had been out trying to make some money. Peaches didn't wanna hear that shit, so she ended the call and then pressed *69. She jotted the number down and decided to call when she got to work. Peaches landed a new job working for Cash Advance. She was a Customer Service Rep and loved her job very much. She made a substantial amount of money and was able to pay all of her bills. After she got to work, she dialed the number, but no one answered. The voicemail came on with a woman's voice, "You just reached Ronda and Shaheed. Sorry we're not here to accept your call. Please leave a message after the beep." Peaches left a message saying, "Shaheed this is Peaches call me back." Later that night, when she got off work, she went home, cooked dinner, and watched a little TV and then her phone rang. "Hello!" she said. In the background, Peaches heard a female yelling in the phone. "Shaheed, who is this Bitch calling my fucking phone? Tell her not to call my house no more." Shaheed didn't say a word. Peaches assumed that it pissed her off even more. The woman started yelling again, "Tell her I'm pregnant, NOW! Tell her!" Shaheed finally picked up the phone and said, "Bitch, don't call here no fucking more!" Before she could even bring herself to respond, he hung up. She didn't know if she wanted to laugh or cry. Was this a joke, or was this just another dog ass Nigga that just lost the best thing that ever happened to him?

Come to find out, Shaheed couldn't be a man and tell Peaches the truth. He wanted out and jumped into another relationship, hoping Peaches would get the message. From the conversation that just happened, she got the message loud and clear. Peaches was stunned at what just went down. Pure anger and rage filled her heart and her mind. The first and only thing that entered her mind was revenge, and she was going to get it one way or another. Nita, Peaches co-worker, had a boyfriend from Griffin. He knew Shaheed, so Peaches asked if he would give her Rhonda's address. Without hesitation, he gave her everything she asked for. On Shaheed's birthday, Peaches went to Ronda's house with her own personal "tools". When she spotted

Shaheed's car, she smeared cake all over the hood of the car. Out of spite, she then took her finger and wrote out the words "Fuck You!" She left the house and rode to the nearest pay phone and dialed Ronda's number. Ronda answered, "Hello!" Peaches responded, "Look outside at your car, Bitch!" and hung the phone up. Six months had passed, and Peaches was doing a good job on maintaining her responsibilities. She even referred to work as "bae." One evening, she clocked out of work, came home, showered, laid on her bed, rolled up a doobie and began to reminisce on the nothing ass Niggas she had come across in her life. Peaches felt as though her precious time had been wasted. She also began to think that maybe she fucked up by not talking to Cap. It had been a while since she had spoken to him. Afterwards, Peaches got up to make some brownies for her munchies when her phone rang. "Hello!" she answered. It was Shaheed, "What's up, Stanky?" he said. Peaches hung up the phone. She was furious with him. Who was he to call and act like he did nothing?

The next morning, Peaches set off to another day at work. When she arrived, she made coffee for her employees and sat at her desk. She looked up saw Shaheed walking towards her. "Since you won't talk to me over the phone, I came to see you in person," he said. Peaches got up and walked outside, "What's up?" she replied nonchalantly. Shaheed replied, "I know your upset and I'm..." Before he could finish, Peaches slapped the shit out of him for playing her like a fool. She walked away with tears in her eyes not wanting to make a scene. With nothing left to say, Shaheed got in his car and left, yet, somehow that wasn't the last of Shaheed. He continued to show up at Peaches' job bringing her lunch and ice cream. He was doing all he could to show Peaches that he was sorry, but she was hurting. That was the longest relationship she had been in. Plus, Peaches was ok with being single; she was pissed that she had even given Shaheed a chance. She had to keep telling herself "you live, and you learn." One Friday night, Peaches was home being a couch potato when her phone rang, and she answered,

"Hello!" "You miss me?" "Who is this?" she replied, "This is Rell," he said. Peaches replied, "How the fuck you get my number, Nigga?!" He laughed and said, "Don't worry about it. What are you doing"? Peaches replied, "None of your business, what you want, Rell?" "Damn, I was just thinking about you and I wanted to check on you," he explained. "Well, I'm ok. Thanks for checking on me," she replied and then hung up. Rell didn't give up. He called Peaches constantly until she gave in. A friend was the only thing Peaches was looking for at the time. Peaches received a call from her mom telling her about how her little sister, Leah, didn't like her school and wanted to come live with Peaches. Annie wanted Peaches to start looking for a two-bedroom apartment because Peaches lived in a one-bedroom apartment.

Her mom helped find a bigger place for the both of them. Leah moved in with Peaches and got a job working at Popeyes. Peaches got off work one evening and stopped by to see Rell. Upon arrival, he already had a doobie rolled up and already for her. Rell was all over Peaches. She exclaimed, "Damn! Nigga can I breathe?" He told Peaches he missed her and while locked up she was all he could think about. Peaches really thought nothing of it. She didn't believe anything Rell said. Two years had passed, and Rell finally won Peaches over. Rell called Peaches asking her to come pick him up. She told him that she was on her way to the mall, so he responded, "Ok, I'll ride with you." When they got to the mall, Peaches was getting frustrated because Rell was rushing her. He said she was spending too much time in one store, so Peaches told Rell he didn't have to come and elaborated on how he invited himself. Plus, she was trying to find her something to wear for that night. She wanted to go out, and Rell was trying to do everything he could to ruin that. After Peaches got to her house, Nita was there waiting on her. They were going to get dressed together. Rell was feeling some kind of way because he wasn't getting any attention from Peaches. He called Peaches' name. Rell was standing in her bedroom. He said, "Why you trying me, Peaches?" She answered, "What are you talking about?"

Rell pulled out a gun and pointed it at Peaches head. For some reason, she wasn't afraid of Rell or his gun. He responded, "I don't want you to go out, but you going any way, huh?" She answered, "Rell, let's go, you're going home." Peaches called Nita's name and told her to ride with her to take Rell home. After they got to Rell's house and dropped him off, Peaches left realizing she had a physco on her hands. Nita suggested they should go to a bar and get "white girl" wasted. When they got to the bar, Peaches rolled a doobie before getting out of the car. Nita rolled the next one, and the both of them were geeked up walking into the bar. Peaches ordered four drinks: two for her and two for Nita. Peaches took a shot every time she thought about how Rell reacted. She couldn't believe it, and she knew for sure Rell was not the one for her. After nearly engulfing her last shot of Patron, she threw up everywhere. Nita had to escort her to the car and drive Peaches home. The moment they got to Peaches' house, she restarted throwing up. This time, the vomiting was non-stop. Leah had to come outside to get Peaches into the house. The next morning, Peaches woke up and found herself laying across her bed. She felt so bad, yet she pondered the question, "Why?"

As much as her and Megan partied before, she never threw up or got sick. She knew, at that moment, something wasn't right and asked Leah to go buy a pregnancy test for her. After taking the test, Peaches cried her eyes out because she knew Rell was the father. She loved Rell, but his temper was going to be a problem.

Chapter 2

"The Mishap"

Peaches wanted more, and she began working for Cash Advance. It was a lovely fall evening and the cool breeze blew through Peaches' long, black, silky hair as she strutted to her car. The maple leaves fell from the trees and their branches were bare against the wind and the cold, wintery light. Once she made it to the bank there were three deposit bags: two money order bags totaling $1500, and a separate bag that had $2500 cash. Peaches grabbed the bags from under her seat, not realizing she only dropped two of the three deposit bags. The third bag was left under the seat. Home was her next destination and she was and excited to be experiencing this beautiful, yet dreadful blessing. P rubbed her stomach as it began to growl, and she stopped by Captain D's and ordered a three-piece, fries, cole slaw, and corn on the cob. Ummm, that was music to her ears as she ordered. While pulling up to her two-bedroom town home she noticed two boys walking out behind her lil sister, Leah, who had just moved in with Peaches. Leah was a junior in high school and asked to use the car to run her friends home? P hesitated for a moment before replying, "Ok! Hurry back." Soon as one of the little fuckers saw the bag that Peaches overlooked, he stuffed it in his pants and remained silent the whole ride home. The next morning Peaches got ready for work, made the drop for her job, and headed to work.

Two days went by before Bank of America called her job stating that a deposit wasn't made. Nita asked Peaches about the drop and she told her that she had did the drop that morning. The bank said they had no trace of the deposit. Peaches didn't know what to think or what was going on because she knew she made the drop. Her supervisor responded by telling her they were going to launch an investigation since the missing deposit was over 3,000 dollars. She was ok with that because she wanted to find out what was going on herself. Three days later, two detectives walked in and asked to speak to Peaches. She introduced herself and told them what happened. She shared with them what time she did the drop, where, and when. One of the detectives was being rude to Peaches and told her that if she didn't tell them where the money was that she was under arrest. Peaches told them the truth. The detective told Peaches to stand up, put her arms behind her back, and she was under arrest. He then began reading her her Miranda Rights, "You have the right to remain silent. Anything you say or do can and will be used against you in a court of law. You have the right to speak to an attorney. If you cannot afford one, one will be provided to you." Peaches was speechless, angry, and afraid - she had never been to jail before. They charged her with theft and after she was processed, she was held with no bond. The first phone call she made was to her mother, and somehow, she had already heard about it. Her next call was Rell. He told Peaches her whole family was threatening him because they assumed he had something to do with what was going on. He then told Peaches he had no idea money was missing, then her phone call had to end. When Peaches returned to her cell, she sat there and begin to cry. She couldn't believe where she was; this place was nasty, smelly, and cold. Jail was not where she expected to be, all she could think about was her baby. Peaches was hungry and began to feel sick and wondered to herself, "WTF is going on?" She was lost and confused because she knew for a fact the drop was made. While sitting there in a daze, she heard her name called and an officer handed her an orange jumpsuit and told her to change her clothes. He then handed her a brown paper bag and instructed her to the put clothes she took off into it. Being naked and feeling violated, she was told to cough and squat. Peaches followed the instructions, then she was sent upstairs to the third floor where she was booked.

Chapter 3

"Screw Up"

Peaches stood as she watched the cell door close. Anxiety started to take control over every inch of her body. The only thing on her mind was the baby. Peaches was three months pregnant, in jail, and confused. Her cellmate introduced herself as "Pooh-baby." She sat and sized Peaches up from her head all the way down to her feet while eating a honeybun. P climbed up on the hard-top bunk and began to cry. She had no idea what was going on. The only thing she knew was that she didn't steal the money. As Peaches laid there, she couldn't get her thoughts together because "Pooh-baby" was snoring loud and it was very annoying. That next morning P sat up and her stomach began to growl. She knew exactly what that meant, the baby was hungry. Her cellmate was up, ready to gossip, and get all up in Peaches' business. "Pooh-baby" began to ask questions such as, "How old are you?" "What are you being charged with?" She could sense P was not used to this type of place and told her everything was gonna be alright. Thank goodness, she heard her name called over the intercom and was told to bring her mat to the front. All of the inmates stood in total shock, they couldn't believe she was going home so soon. P was escorted to court and stood in front of the judge not knowing what was going to happen next. Peaches was overwhelmed with joy to see her parents there supporting her, it gave her heart a warm feeling. Standing handcuffed in front of the judge, P felt hopeless and everything was running through her mind, "Should I tell the judge I didn't do it?" "What should I do?" "What should I say?" The judge granted her bail and she stood in disbelief. P was awakened by the slamming of the gavel. Still in a daze, she tried to pull her shit together, but her legs were getting weaker and weaker the longer she stood. An officer handed her the brown paper bag with her belongings. P got out of that ugly ass orange jumpsuit, got dressed, and headed to the front to be released. Once Peaches stepped foot outside of the jail, she couldn't help to think revenge is the best dish served cold. But right now, all she could focus on was getting home and having a hot meal. She wasn't locked up long, but it was still too long. She missed freedom. Now, with a full, happy bell, she was ready for a bath. Soaking her ass felt so good. She sat in the tube for about an hour and pondering how this could have happened to her. Peaches' phone rang, and the caller id read "Unknown Caller" so she ignored it. Two minutes later, it rang again "Unknown Caller" appeared and she answered, "Hello!" There was silence. "HELLO!" she yelled. "Ummm," the caller responded and then he cleared his throat before he said, "They're going around saying they hit a lick." Peaches heard a dial tone and sat up. She knew what that meant, but who the fuck was that anonymous caller? Whoever it was, they confirmed what Peaches already knew. She was very popular in school and a lot of guys fucked with her hard just because of how authentic she was. Peaches was always dressed to impress, was quiet, and very low key; a lot of Niggas loved that about her. So, whoever the caller was felt that it was right to put her on to what was being said in the streets. Peaches never had conflicts with anybody and if she did, it was rare, and everyone knew it. Once Leah got home, P asked, "Where them Niggas live at?" Come to find out, karma came back around a year later and clapped one of dem Nigga's ass two, he was killed: two gunshot wounds to the chest. They say he was at the wrong place at the wrong time. He was keeping a low profile, no one had seen or heard from him since Peaches' sentencing. The streets were talking tho. His partner in crime, her sister's boyfriend, was still around. He had the nerve to try to apologize to Peaches one day. Sayin' he didn't mean for her to go to jail and pleaded with Peaches to not tell the police he stole the money. He wasn't worried about Peaches, he was worried about that contract he had just signed with MOMONEY$RECORDS.

But, at the end of the day Peaches couldn't be mad at any one but herself for being careless. Thank God her job didn't show up for court! And because they didn't, the charges were dropped. She wasn't off completely scott free, she was sentenced to 1 year of community service. Peaches had to plead guilty due to the amount. Since this was her first time ever going to jail, she was told it was best to plea under the First Offender Act. Peaches was pissed because she couldn't prove that the money was stolen, so she decided to let nature take its course, you will reap what you sow!

Three months had passed, and it was a rainy Saturday evening, and Peaches decided to lounge around the house and chill. She was trying to gather her thoughts, "hmm" as she began to think. P never really spoke about how she felt, her actions said it best. As Peaches reached for her phone, a smile came across her face as she dialed his number. "Yoo!" he answered. Peaches had a request for him and told him, "I'll text you the location and we'll go from there." Then, text me after you're done." This mysterious man responded, "10-4," and the call ended.

The mystery man was "Money." He handled all of Peaches' dirty laundry. Money made sure she was protected and if anybody fucked with her, she knew to call. Peaches texted Money the 411 Leah gave her. Later that night, Peaches was lying in bed, looking up at the ceiling. It was so quiet you could hear a pin drop. Her heart began to beat rapidly, sadness and sorrow seemed to be flooding her. Then, to herself, she yelled, out, "Fuck it! Why should I give a Fuck?" Peaches didn't want to feel sorry, nor did she care about what was about to happened. All kinds of scenarios ran through her head. Her anxiety was on high and she wanted to know what was taking so long? She tossed and turned all night. She woke up the next morning to the thundering sounds of moaning and banging from her neighbors fucking. "Ughhhh," she sighed, you would've thought they were trying to kill each other the way they were going at it. Peaches had her broom within reach and beat the ceiling to death. Five minutes later, she received a call from her neighbor, Cody, apologizing. "You still a hoe, I see," Peaches replied. He chuckled. Peaches knew how he got down, he had a different girl every day of the week. And then Peaches told him, "Keep that shit down." "Girl you know you want this dick stop flexing!" he responded. "Boy, bye!" Peaches hung up on his ass.

While sitting home surfing the net, Peaches ran across a job posting she was interested, it was a medical records clerk position. Shortly after she applied, she received an email to arrive the very next morning for an interview. "Yes!" Peaches exclaimed. She decided to get dressed and find something nice to wear for her interview but before she could get into the shower, there was a knock at the door. She grabbed her robe and went to see who it was. "Who is it?" She looked through the peep hole and noticed it was Lil Johnny from next door; he was so cute and had the biggest crush on Peaches. She opened the door, "Hey Johnny!" He just smiled and said, "Are you ready for me to take your trash?" Peaches forgot what day it was, "Hold on! Let me get it for you." She grabbed 5 dollars out of her purse before heading back to the door. As P headed back to pay Johnny she heard her phone ringing from her room, hoping they didn't hang up she dived on her bed and grabbed the phone, "Hello!" "Was up?" it was Rell." He sounded different. "I'm in the hospital," he continued by saying his leg was broken but everything else was minor. "Are you ok?" Peaches was concerned. She heard in his voice that he was in pain. She then asked, "Who was with you?" He hesitated, but then responded, "My home girl was driving." "Oh! Ok!" Peaches continued, "Is she ok?" "Yeah, she good, imma call u right back," click. Well damn, Peaches thought when she heard the dial tone. "Rude ass!" she mumbled. Rell and Peaches was more like oil and water. She was only 17 when she met him. Now that she's older, she realizes everything isn't always as good as it looks.

Chapter 4

Loyalty & Lies

October 23, 2006 was a pinnacle day for Peaches. She gave birth to a beautiful, 7 lb 6-ounce baby girl, and named her Lola. She hoped things would work out between her and Rell, but she couldn't handle his temperament. She knew staying with him for the sake of the baby was wrong and it wouldn't be healthy for her new baby girl. Lola was 6 months old when P found out Rell had another baby on the way. The chicken head's name is Ricka and she was the one in the car accident with him when he called Peaches from the hospital. This hoe was straight from the projects. She was both ghetto and ratchet at the same damn time. Rell would trap out her house all day and then run to Peaches for a good night's rest. Ricka knew exactly where she stood. She knew his heart really belonged to Peaches and she hated it. She followed him to Peaches' house one night to let it be known that she was pregnant. Now why in the fuck would she wanna go and do that? Peaches heard a loud commotion outside and when she looked out of the window, it was this Bitch. She was screaming Ricka to the top of her lungs, "Go get that Bitch! I'll tell her myself!" It was at that moment Rell knew he fucked up. That night was the night Peaches found out Ricka was pregnant. Peaches didn't give a fuck if the Bitch was pregnant or not, all knew was that that hoe better not come knocking on her door. As far as she was concerned, Rell didn't need to knock either, he needed to go back home with her. She could hoop and holla all night, Peaches really didn't care. She realized that night, being with him wasn't the move anyway; she wasn't hard up for no man. She hated the fact that she had even given this man the time of day. Now she wondered about Cap and what he was doing these days. He never meant her any harm and he really did care for Peaches. She was beautiful, her mahogany skin was as smooth as a Hershey's

Chocolate Bar. When she went anywhere, she was well coordinated. If she had on a mink coat, she'd sport the mink. One morning while dropping Lola off at the sitter, before going to work, she stopped to get gas, and out of nowhere this guy asked if he could pump for her? Peaches giggled and got back into her all white, 2009 Ford F-250 and waited until he finished. After he hung the pump he knocked on her window and asked if she needed anything else? Peaches replied, "I'll take a soda pop." P watched him through the rear-view mirror as he walked off. His muscles were defined, and his veins stuck out, emphasizing his strengths. When he returned back to the car he handed Peaches two sodas. She thanked him and as she was about to pull off, he said, "I seen you watching me. You keep looking at me like that, you gone make me kidnap you." Peaches sped off fast as hell but when she heard him screaming, "Aye, Aye, Aye, Ayeee" she stopped. He was hopping on one foot yelling, "You ran over my foot!" Peaches put her car in reverse and then got out to see if he was ok. This dude had the nerve to be sizing her up from head to toe. He thought she was the most beautiful woman he'd ever laid eyes on. He began to laugh once he saw the concerned look on Peaches' face. POW! She slapped his ass. "Don't you ever play with me like that, Fool!" Peaches proclaimed, as she continued to beat the shit outta him. He just laughed and blocked every punch she threw at him. "OK!" he replied, "I just couldn't let you go that easily." "What you mean?" Peaches screamed, as she continued to look at him like he was crazy as hell. "Baby, please, can I have your number," he asked? "Hell naw!" Peaches replied, as she got back in her truck, "Nigga, you out here playing and got me late for work. What the fuck is wrong with you?" P Snapped. "Besides, I don't even know your name. What do I look like giving a stranger my number?" Eazy just smiled and said, "Hi! I'm Eazy! I think I love you already." To him, Peaches was like love at first sight, he wasn't used to a woman like P. He was fine after all,, so she gave up the digits.

Two years later, Peaches was now living in Midtown, Atlanta, Ga. She just received her business license for catering. She always wanted to start her own business and her time was finally here. Peaches was now one of the hottest celebrity caterers in the city and hosting all of the biggest events. Everything was now falling into place. Giving Eazy a chance felt good, he loved her and Lola. Every time she pulled up on him she couldn't wait to put her lips against his skin and maybe even suck his collar bone.

Eazy was five years older than P and he catered to her. "Here, I got you something," Eazy handed her two new gold bracelets to add to her collection, "Thank you, Baby" Peaches replied. She loved jewelry, and he knew that it would melt her heart. Fast money and living the fast life were all Eazy knew; for some reason, P was always attracting street niggas. She noticed something different about him: he had potential but was lacking ambition. P was willing to help in that area. Ever since they met, he had been there for Lola like she was his. P appreciated him for that because being a single parent was hard as hell. Rell was pissed that Peaches didn't want his ass, but taking it out on Lola was gonna kill him in the long run.

It was a hot summer day and Eazy and Peaches had just left church. As soon as they got home, he prepared Sunday Dinner for Peaches and Lola they both decided to be couch potatoes for the rest of the day. Dressing, yams, baked chicken, and rice was on the menu; Eazy could cook his ass off. P loved how he catered to her. What she hated though was the fact that he took care of home all day and was in the streets all night. She suggested for him to enroll in school for Culinary Arts. Eazy was so used to the fast money that the shit Peaches was talking was going through one ear and out the other. The doorbell rang, "I got it, Bae!" Eazy replied. He pressed the intercom, Yooo! Heyyyy, its Tori, Nigga." Once they made it upstairs she ran to Lola and planted a kiss on her forehead. Toby came in behind her, gave Peaches a hug, and slapped fives with Eazy. They brought Lola two pair of Gucci shoes. She was so spoiled by Eazy and Peaches that it was ridiculous. Tori and Toby had been together for about ten years. Toby owned two barbershops and a nail salon. He took very good care of Tori. She was blessed and didn't know it. The bitch never had to work, all she had to do was make sure the house was cleaned and dinner was served. She couldn't do that to save her hoe life. Tori was a hoe and her pussy was for everybody. Dinner was now ready. During dinner, Tori asked to be excused from the table; she went to the bathroom and stayed forever; only God knows what the hell was going on in there. Tori finally made her way back to the table. "Damn, you ok?" Toby asked Tori sounding sarcastic. Eazy got up from the table, grabbed a bottle of Ace of Spades and four glasses and then poured everyone drinks. Toby and Eazy were having a little dispute about the football game, Alabama vs. Georgia. They were beginning to get so loud that if frightened Lola. Peaches wasn't really into making friends with Tori, there was something about her, but she couldn't put her hands on. "Yea I'm straight," she replied. "Where we going tonight?" Tori asked? She always stayed in somebody's club trying to trail behind her brother. Eazy was well known in the streets and his sista, Tori knew it. She was a low down, dirty, gold digging ass bitch that was down for whatever. Eazy told Tori, "Me & Toby going to the "Goldroom," but you not! Tori never argued with her brother, but you could tell she was in her feelings. After everyone ate, Peaches cleaned the kitchen and closed shop, it was Lola's bedtime. Once she fell asleep, Eazy and Peaches cuddled on the sofa. These two love birds were inseparable, and everyone knew it. "Awww, so what, y'all in love now? My brother's in love, that's so cute" Tori said, sounding a bit disgusted. Eazy laughed, but Peaches didn't, it sounded as if Tori was hating a little bit. Peaches wasn't pressed about it though. Toby's phone kept going off, so he told Eazy he was about to go home so he could get ready for the night. Peaches always made sure her man looked good when he went out and tonight was no different. She pulled out his Pucc Leovono's jeans with a Pucc T-shirt to match. Peaches told him not to be out too late and to hurry back so he could beat her pussy into a coma. Eazy laughed and shook his head before responding, "Yes, Ma'am!" Once he left, Peaches made sure everything was prepped for the very next day. She had 50 clients to serve for a fashion event being held at the W Hotel. Afterwards, she showered and decided to send her cousin Megan a text, "Hey Cousin, we need to link up for a girl's night out." Then her phone rang, she saw it was Eazy calling, "Hello!" she answered. "STOP! You tripping," is what she heard on the other end. It was Eazy's voice, but Peaches couldn't figure out who he was talking too. "HELLO!" "HELLO!" P replied, but she got no response. Peaches hung up and sent a text, "You ok, Baby?" About ten minutes had passed before she received a response from Eazy saying that he was ok and inquired why she asked. She replied, "Your phone pocket dialed me. Who was you talking too?" Eazy responded quickly, "Oh, that was this Nigga name Red. He owes me some money; everything's good." "Oh, ok, Baby, just making sure. "I Love You." she replied. Eazy then replied, "I Love You Too!" They ended the call, she rolled over, and was out like a light. The next morning, Peaches rolled over to Eazy snoring like a pig, "Ewwww," Peaches mushed his head, kissed him, got out of bed, and was ready to start her day. She got dressed and then went to wake Lola the Princess, she was everything to Peaches. "Rise and shine," she said as she opened Lola's blinds before picking her up. It took no time to get Lola ready. Peaches decided to take her to the sitter and would come back to pack for the event. When she got back home, Peaches heard Eazy's phone ringing, it was Tori. Peaches wondered what she could possibly want this early in the morning and why the fuck she wasn't sleep. Peaches then thought maybe Toby didn't come home last night. In the back of her mind she thought Toby had better taste than that. Tori wasn't a bad looking woman, but who was Peaches to judge? Toby was fine as hell; he was tall and built like LLCoolJ, he had nice skin, was always well groomed, and could dress his ass off. Peaches knew Tori was only in it for the money. He was more laid back and too well-mannered for Tori.

She was an alley cat that could dress, pull men, and could suck a mean dick. Her name was ringing in the streets and Eazy knew it. Peaches wondered sometimes if Eazy was ashamed to know that his sista was a hoe. Eazy woke up and realized Peaches wasn't in the bed. "Bae, where you at"? he shouted. "Why, you miss me?" Peaches shouted back? "You know dat," Eazy shot back. Peaches walked back to bed and got under the covers and sucked Eazy's soul out his body. He moaned so loud Peaches had to cover his mouth. "Damn, Baby!" Eazy whispered, he then turned Peaches over and pound her kitty to death. He was fucking her so good they both was shedding tears after they were done. Eazy kissed her forehead, pulled out his wallet, and handed her

2,000 dollars. He told her to have a good day and she responded with, "Thank You, Baby!" They both got dressed and Eazy packed her truck and made sure she had everything before taking off. Once Peaches got in her truck, blew Eazy a kiss, and then popped in Otgenasis, "Push It." Her speakers were thumpin' so loud, P was beatin' the block down. For the most part, everything was going well, and Peaches was having a pleasant day so far. Once she arrived, an employee was there to help her unload. Within an hour, all of the tables were set, the utensils were laid out neatly, from the forks to the spoons, knives, plates, napkins and glasses. The decorations were outstanding. Peaches had to step back to take a good look at what she had put together all by herself. She loved working alone, it was soothing for her. The menu read: dressing, mashed potatoes, green beans, buttered rolls, and smothered pork chops. Champagne from Ace of Spades, Dom Perignon, to Krug. Peaches made sure everyone was well feed and comfortable before she excused herself to check on Lola. When she called, the sitter informed her that it was nap time and to call back in an hour. A camera man approached Peaches and asked if he could take her picture. She was proud of all that she had accomplished. When it came to her work, she was organized, and a beast at what she did. Peaches saw a text from Megan saying that a girl's night out was well needed and that she would call her later. As soon as Peaches was done, she decided to stop by Ford to see if she could trade her truck in; she needed more room for work. Eazy had called just in time, P told him what she wanted to do and he told her to take her time and choose carefully. It was going to take him 30 minutes to get there and he didn't want her to make a final decision until after he arrived. When Eazy arrived, he approached Peaches with a hug while taking a big chunk of her ass, "Hey, Baby!" Peaches then planted a kiss on his neck. "Have you decided what you wanted?" he asked. Peaches was very indecisive when it came to making up here mind, "Yeah, I'll take that one right there," she pointed to the new Ford F-150 with the super crew cab, V-6 cyl, with black on black leather interior. She loved trucks for some reason. Whatever his baby wanted, he made sure to make it happen. After they left the dealership, Eazy told Peaches to meet him up the street, he had a taste for some ribs from *This Is It*. As they pulled up Eazy got out, "Bae, you want something out of here?" Peaches wasn't paying attention, she was too busy learning how to program her playlist; she loved music. "Bae!" He was now at her window to get her undivided attention. "I'm sorry, Baby, what you say?" "You hungry?" Eazy asked? "Naw, I'm good," Peaches responded. She kissed him before saying, "I'm about to go get Lola. I'll meet you at the house. What time will you be home, Baby?" Eazy looked at his Roley, "I can't give you an exact time, but I promise you, it won't be late." Peaches rolled her eyes and told him not to be late before pulling off. Later that night, she put Lola to bed and was ready for Eazy to get home. She was going to give it to him good tonight. She had Jay Holiday playing and made sure her pole was intact. This was an exclusive show; she was all about pleasing her man. When Eazy walked in the house he called out for her, "Bae!" The first thing he saw when he walked into the bedroom was the pole. Now smiling from ear to ear he shouted, "Damn, Baby, where you at?" Peaches was hiding, waiting for Eazy to get relaxed. "Damn, Baby, I don't have no ones, but I got some Benjamin Franklins," he laughed, "Where you at?" "C'mon, Baby, come on out, I can't wait." Eazy was excited like a kid waiting to open their gifts on Christmas Day. Peaches walked out while *Falsetto* was playing by the Dream. She strutted out with her red bottoms, a red see-through body suit, and worked the pole like a pro. Peaches knew how to dance, but only kept her moves in the bedroom for man. Eazy laid back on the bed, biting his lip, and while throwing those Benjis at her, he told her, "Baby, you can have whatever you want." She dropped down and began to grind her ass slowly. Eazy got up to get a better look. "Omg, Baby, don't stop," he said, "I love you, Baby!" Peaches never responded, she remained silent while making her man go crazy. She didn't get to finish, Eazy couldn't resist. He got down on the floor with Peaches and began to caress her body, then he ripped her body suit in half and made love to her until the sun came up.

Chapter 5

Love Triangle

It was Christmas Day, 2014, and Eazy had made plans to take Peaches out that night. Dinner was at Peaches' mother's house. There were family members she hadn't seen in years sitting at the table. Megan and Peaches were able to catch up on old times and with their cousin NeNe there, it seemed like a mini family reunion. Peaches noticed Eazy's facial expression as he stepped outside to take a call. "Baby, what's wrong?" He responded, "Nothing, Baby! That was just Tori, she wanted to know if she could pull up?" Peaches hesitated and thought that was kinda weird Tori wanted to come by because her and Tori wasn't close like that. Eazy saw the look on Peaches' face and told her that Tori said Toby was getting on her nerves and that she needed a break, so she wanted to know if she could chill with us? Peaches shrugged her shoulders and told him it was ok as she walked off. It didn't take long for Tori to arrive and the fam treated her with some great southern hospitality making her feel right at home. Lola was staying with Peaches' mom for the night, so she was going to hang out with Mo. Debating on what she was going to wear that night, she sent a text Mo, "What we are wearing tonight?" She texted back, "I don't know yet, P! It's only 7:15pm, we got time to decide. All they had to do was open their closets, it was full of designer wear. Peaches' phone rang and saw it was Rell, "Yeah!" she answered. "Don't be answering the phone like that. Where's my baby? You acting brand new since you got a Nigga now, huh?" Peaches told him, "Don't be calling my phone with that bullshit. Your child is good! You know I'm not asking you for shit. You don't do shit for her anyways, so stay the fuck off my phone." "Yo ass is mine!" was the response. He hung up and didn't call back. They were dressed to impress: Peaches wore black leather pants, a short-fitted sweater, with fur around the collar, and a pair of black, Gucci boots, with fur around the ankle. Her diamonds were dripping. Eazy was drippin' too. He was iced out with a black fur, black slacks, and the gators Peaches got him for Christmas, gold Rolex, and diamond earrings with a gold, iced out ring to match. While getting dressed, they grooved to Teddy Pendergrass, "*Practice What You Preach.*" Mo called P to ask what time she was leaving and to confirm they were all meeting at the Gold Room about 11:30. P told her, "Yes!" and for her to call as soon as she pulled up.

Eazy decided they would style and profile, so he drove his all black 2015 Porsche. When they finally got there, Tori called her brother asking if they were inside yet. Peaches didn't even know that he invited her to come and hang out with them. It was like another family reunion, once they walked in, it seemed as if all of Peaches' cousins were in the building too. Her cousin, NeNe, and her husband, Mr. Brown, were already lit and everyone was waiting on P, so they could all turn up together.

Eazy reserved a VIP section and that shit was packed to the capacity. They had waitresses bring bottles out left and right while the photographer was taken hella pictures, nonstop. The DJ was playing all the latest hits. She was having so much fun, she hadn't noticed Toby and Tori walk in. Not to mention, she was busy giving Eazy the best lap dance he ever had. When she looked up, she noticed Tori standing next to Eazy, she couldn't believe this Bitch didn't even speak. P didn't worry about it because she just wanted to have a good time, but every time she turned around she caught Tori whispering in Eazy's ear. Now she was paying more attention to the bitch; Peaches knew she was up to something no good.

Eazy grabbed Peaches by her waist and she started to grind on him, he followed suite, and they danced all night. P noticed Toby and Tori dancing too, but caught Tori watching them all while giving Peaches the side eye. She was dancing with Toby like she was trying to outdo her brother. Tori saw P looking at her and flicked her one. Peaches wasn't sure if she saw what she thought she saw, so just to make sure, she flicked her one back. As Peaches turned her back, Eazy had dropped down on one knee with a Noori, 14k Gold 3ct ring. It was shining bright like the smile on her face. The DJ stopped the music, "Baby, will you be my wife?" "Yes! Yes! Yes!" Peaches screamed. The whole fuckin' club went bananas. He put the ring on her finger, they kissed, and P hugged him so tight she almost choked the man to death. She was excited her family was there to experience this night with her; it sure was a night to remember. Her cousins congratulated both of them, it was so swwweeet. Peaches was on cloud 9 and she couldn't wait to show her parents and her sista.

That next morning, she woke up to breakfast in bed along with a dozen roses; the man of her life was finally here to rescue her and Lola. He cooked her pancakes, grits, eggs, sausage, with a side of fruit, and a glass of good ole cold OJ. Eazy was putting on his coat and told Peaches someone was waiting on him at the park up the street (she automatically knew what that meant). He kissed P and told her he would be right back, and to enjoy her breakfast. Peaches couldn't wait to call her mom, as she was dialing her number, she heard a knock at the door. "Who is it?" she yelled. "It's me, Rell." The last time she had spoken to him, their conversation wasn't pleasant at all. She looked through the peep hole and noticed he had a bag full of stuff for Lola, was debating whether or not to open the door. "Mannn, damn, P! "How long you gone have me standing out here?" She shot back, "Nigga, you should've called first!" she responded as she opened the door. But as soon as she opened the door, Rell charged at Peaches causing her to fall to the floor. "Get the fuck off me, Rell!" she screamed. "Yeah, that Nigga ain't here to save you now, huh?" Peaches wrestled with him until he got tired. Then he laughed and mushed her face before getting up and walking through the house. "Where my baby?" Before he knew it, Peaches was right behind his ass with a 9mm and slapped his bitch ass across the head; he fell to the floor unconscious. Peaches called Eazy and got no answer. She dialed 911. Rell took this to far, she was sick of his ass. When the police came, they took his black ass to jail. P was a little shook and she still couldn't reach Eazy. She panicked, thinking something went wrong. Being the "ride or die" that she was, she jumped in her truck and drove to the park where he was. By this time, it was about 1:00pm and no one was at the park and it was easy for her to spot Eazy's car. But then she saw Tori's car, so she slowed down and parked where she couldn't be seen. She began dialing Eazy's number while walking towards Tori's car. Peaches was on some stealth like shit. She was walking between trees and bushes, you might of thought she was working for the FBI the way she was trying to investigate. Shaking her head as she got closer thinking to herself, "I knew this nothing ass bitch was cheating on Toby." Peaches saw Tori giving head to some guy but couldn't seem to grasp it from where she was standing. "Ugh," Peaches thought, she just had to get closer to get a better look, this shit was beginning to get juicy. This made her forget about the little bullshit she just went through with Rell. As Peaches got closer, she thought about how Eazy always told her to protect herself at all times, so she decided to go back to her car grab her pistol before going any further. As Peaches headed back towards Tori's care, her heart was beating. The closer she got, the faster her heart beat. She could see Tori sucking somebody husband's dick like an oxtail bone; that's all she was good for. "Is that who I think it?" Peaches said out loud? The guy was getting head on the passenger side while she was sitting between his legs. He was caught off guard because his eyes were closed with his head was tilted back. Eazy didn't know what was coming. Peaches tapped on the driver side window with her pistol. Tori screamed and after opening his eyes, Eazy pushed her off of him and jumped out of the car. "Y'all nasty ass fuck! Ain't y'all siblings? Naw, y'all can't be. I knew there was something about you, Bitch," as she aimed the pistol at Tori's head.

Eazy shouted, "Baby, please let me explain!" He then pulled his gun out of his pants aimed and it at his head. Peaches screamed, "NOO!" He then turned the gun on Tori and tears began to roll down her face, "15 years gone down the drain just like that, huh?" she said. Eazy screamed, "Shut up, Bitch! Baby, please don't listen to her." Eazy insisted, "she's not my sister, she's just my hoe. Tori works for me I came here to dismiss her -- POW! POW!

"So, Tori was selling pussy?" She said out loud, it all made sense now. Peaches wanted to break down, but now wasn't the time. Tori was lying there with blood leaking from her chest and her head. "Why did you do this to me, Eazy? How could you do this to me? How could you go from sugar to shit?" Eazy told her, "Now is not the time, Peaches! I'll explain later." Eazy wanted to shit on his self, he was afraid he was next. "Yo, those gun shots didn't come from your gun Peaches! Who'd you bring with you, Peaches? Peaches stop playing!" as he tried to take charge of the situation. Again, he asked, "Who else is in on this? I promise you, when I find out..." Peaches cut him off, "You ain't gone do shit, Nigga! Now, let's go, it's my time to play!" and she motioned the gun towards her car telling. As Eazy walked to the car, she still had the gun aimed at him. Trying to sweet talk his way of out of this he says, "Baby, you love me too much to shoot me." Peaches than pointed the gun towards his feet --POW! Eazy shouted real loud, "PEACHES!!!" "Don't ever underestimate me! Get yo ass in the trunk!" "What?" Eazy shouted, "you got me fucked up." She clapped his ass with the gun. "I said GET IN THE FUCKING TRUNK!" When Eazy saw Peaches wasn't bullshittin', he did what he was told. "Baby, let me explain I ... I.." Peaches slammed the trunk and gave a signal to her hittas. Eazy knew Peaches had help with whatever the situation may have been, she was well respected in the streets and her face card was good anywhere. Her phone rang, and the caller said, "I Got You!" It was the same caller that handled the other situation; it was Money. "Thanks, Bro." Eazy could hear Peaches on the phone, but couldn't map out who she was talking to. "Where is she taking me?" he wondered, full of fright. "This woman has gone crazy, God please help me," he prayed. Once Peaches arrived home, she pulled into the garage, popped the trunk open, and told stupid to get out. "We're better than this, Bae!" With pure anger, she told him, "You see where she at, right?" "I was choosing you, Babe! That bitch is dead! Now, you don't have anything to worry about." Eazy began walking towards Peaches, she began walking backwards, slowly, and boldly shouted, "Hold both hands in the air!" They ended up in their bedroom, "Sit!" Peaches said, as she reached for her handcuffs. She then threw them at Eazy and said, "You know what to do." She kept the gun aimed at Eazy's head and by this time, he knew Peaches wasn't fucking around. Peaches didn't say much, she just sat and looked at Eazy in disgust. "You make me sick Nigga!" Eazy was now handcuffed to the bed, but Peaches couldn't sit still. She had too much shit running through her mind and she had to think quick. The room was quiet. As Eazy sat there in silence, Peaches stood pondering her next move. She took her phone out of her pocket and began dialing. Eazy's eyes got big, "Baby, who you calling?" Peaches ignored every word he said. "Hey, Bro, wassup?" Eazy wanted to know who she was on the phone with, but he was too afraid to ask. Peaches put the phone on speaker and then said," Eazy would like to tell you something." She called his homeboy, Toby. "Aye, bro! You ok?" Toby asked. "I'm sorry, my brother," Eazy replied. He dropped his head before speaking, "I betrayed you. Tori's not my sister, she's been a worker for me for years now. I... I..." Eazy was getting choked up, he felt bad for not keeping it real with his homeboy. He continued, "I was telling Tori that I couldn't do this any longer and that holding this secret was eating me up on the inside. She begged me not to tell and offered me some head. Even though it was wrong, I let her do it; I was thinking with the wrong head. I was gonna come clean today, not only to Peaches, but to you as well. I'm sorry bro." "Well, bro, even though you fucked up, I still love you, my Nigga!"

Toby replied, "I knew that bitch wasn't shit since day one. I felt something wasn't right between y'all, but imma keep it real with you though Eazy, I told Peaches it was just a matter of time before it came out. I'm not even mad at you but, I can't trust you." Nothing but silence followed, you could hear a pin drop. Tears began to fall down Eazy's face. Because of this, he just lost his ace, and his soon to be wife, who was the love of his life. Peaches didn't care about his tears, she slid her engagement ring off and threw it at Eazy. Then she shouted, "WHY???" He was caught red handed, there was nothing he could say that would make Peaches feel any better, so he just remained silent. "Ding Dong!" Peaches wasn't expecting any company, who could this be? She told Eazy if he made a sound he was dead. Eazy was surprised, it was Toby. "Bro, please, let's all just talk." Eazy pleaded. But while he pleaded, Peaches started taking off her clothes. "Aye!! What the fuck is going on?" Eazy Shouted? Peaches nor Toby said a word. Toby pushed Peaches' head up against the wall while gently caressing her ass, and then put his hand in between her thighs to spread her legs apart. "Please, please don't make me watch this!" Eazy cried out, Please...!" Toby pulled his long hard wood out, pressed it up against Peaches ass, and politely made his way into her vajaja. She began to moan with every stroke. This made Eazy cried even harder. "I'm sorry, Babe! Can y'all please stop?" Eazy almost lost his mind. He couldn't stand to watch anymore and closing his eyes didn't make it any easier; hearing Peaches moan made it worse. Toby whispered in Peaches' ear, "Do you want me to stop?" She insisted, "Keep going, they played us Toby! They been fucking for 15 years. Then she yelled, "Faster!" and Toby rammed his dick in Peaches even harder; he always wanted to know what that pussy felt like. Eazy was beside himself and began to kick and scream. He was so pissed, his veins were about to burst out his neck, he thought he was gonna have a heart attack. Toby pulled up his pants, looked at Eazy, and said, "I guess we're even now, Bro!" and then he walked out.

Five days later was Tori's funeral. From what the streets were saying, she committed suicide. Eazy blew the horn when he arrived, but Peaches really didn't want to attend. But she also didn't want to look suspicious either. The whole ride, neither spoke a one word to each other. Eazy was still sick from the other, day he didn't know if he was going or coming. Once they arrived, Eazy got out to open Peaches' door. She didn't even wait for him to close it before she started walking, leaving Eazy behind. Knowing she was the cause of Tori's death didn't bother Peaches one bit. She didn't even go up to view the body. Peaches spotted Toby, he was with his mother. Toby and Eazy made eye contact but didn't greet each other. The ceremony was short and full lot of her sugar daddies. These attentive, old ass men she should've been ashamed of themselves. The man of Tori's dreams was right in front of her, and she was too blind to see it, "What a dummy!" Peaches thought. Same shit different toilet, Eazy was in the same boat as she was, two stupid dogs.

Chapter 6

"Monster In Disguise"

Four years later, Lola was excited and couldn't wait for Santa to bring her a new bike. This is what she wanted for Christmas. Peaches and Lola were finishing baking chocolate chip cookies for Santa when the phone rang, "Hello! Merry Christmas!" it was Peaches' father. "Hey, Dad, how are you?" "I'm ok," he replied, "How's my grandbaby?" He hadn't seen Lola in a while. "She's good. Dad, my baby's four years old now." Walter was Peaches' father; he just moved to Georgia recently, so he could spend more time with his kids and Lola. "I'll be over tomorrow to drop off your Christmas gifts." Peaches told him that was fine and that she'll see him then. After ending the call, the doorbell rang, "Who is it?" Peaches yelled. "Open up, its me, your mother!" She picked up Lola's Christmas gifts from

Rell, he could no longer step foot near Peaches after the shit he pulled years ago. He had visitation rights to see Lola every other weekend, but he had to pick her up and drop her off at Peaches' mom's house. Once she saw the gifts, she couldn't wait for bedtime, Christmas Day wasn't coming soon enough.

Peaches just purchased a new house that had five bedrooms and she was neighbors with Cardi B and Offset. So, to celebrate, Christmas dinner was at Peaches' house and she had everything on the fuckin' menu. There was so much food you could feed the homeless. Her mother was shocked asking, "P, who's gonna eat all this?" "Ma, you know our family is huge and all of 'em greedy. I promise this food will not go to waste," while chuckling. Her sister Leah was also coming over and everyone decided to spend the night so they could enjoy seeing Lola open her gifts in the morning. The very next morning, everybody was up extra early and watched Lola open everything in sight.

Peaches had Christmas music playing and breakfast was being served. Peaches was anxious to see her father, it had been so long since they talked. He was pissed when Peaches went to jail a few years ago when her sister's dumb ass boyfriend stole the cash drop bag out of her car. He couldn't believe how careless she was for that to even happen, but he was relieved the charges were dropped and that his daughter wasn't a thief. It's now 4:00pm and so many people were coming and going all night. Life was pretty good for Peaches and her career had taken off like a rocket, to include the purchase of a restaurant that was used for her catering business. Walter finally arrived and both Leah and Peaches were excited to see him. Their mom, however, couldn't stand the ground he walked on and he knew it. But Walter he didn't care, Lola was his main concern and he held her the whole time he was there. They enjoyed each other's company all night. After Peaches' mom left, Leah, Walter and Peaches stayed up reminiscing on the good times they had growing up. Walter asked P if it was ok if he spent the night. "Of course, it's ok, Pops," she replied. Lola was all worn out and knocked out cold, so Peaches put her to bed. Leah gave hugs and before leaving told her dad she'd be over in the morning. Once the house was clear, Peaches starting cleaning and made sure Walter was comfortable. Once everything was in order, she headed to her room to relax before calling it a night. After showering, Lola crossed Peaches' mind, so went to check on her princess. When she got down the hall, she noticed Lola's door was cracked open. Through the crack, she saw her dad standing over Lola. She wasn't sure what to make out of what she was seeing so she just stood and watched. She couldn't believe her eyes and tears started falling. Walter had one of Lola's legs up in the air, but she remained dead asleep. Peaches wanted to see exactly what he was about to do, so she watched and waited. He was just watching her lay there. Peaches didn't want to wake Lola, so she softly said, "What the fuck are you doing?" He dropped her leg and tried to run out of the room. Peaches tripped his ass and his old ass fell to the floor, head first. She ran to her room and grabbed a pair of hand cuffs, cuffed him, pistol whipped him until all she saw was blood. Peaches dragged him into her bathroom, so Lola couldn't see what was going on. She ran to check if her baby had been touched because at this point, she didn't know what to think nor did she know who this man was in her house. This wasn't her father, couldn't be. She didn't know what to think, there was no way he was going to do what she thought he was going to do. Not to her little Princess, his granddaughter, really? Peaches began to pace back and forth and contemplated whether or not she should she call 9-1-1. Walter began moaning but couldn't talk because Peaches duck taped his mouth. She removed the tape and pointed the 9mm to his head, "What were you about to do to my child?" she asked. Walter started to explain, "SLAP!" The gun went across his head and blood splattered everywhere. "Please don't kill me!" Walter cried out. All she could say was, "Fuck you! So, you a molester now, Nigga?" She had so many questions, she just kept telling herself to think. She had to clean this shit up. As Peaches cleaned, he watched and cried even harder. Furiously she asked, "So, what, you used to touch on me and my sister too, Nigga?" "SLAP" She hit his ass again. Checking on Lola to make sure she was still asleep put her at ease. "God, forgive me for what I'm about to do," she prayed out loud. Peaches put the silencer on the 9mm and Walter began to recite The Lord's Prayer: "Our father, who art in heaven, hallowed be thy name, thy kingdom come, thy will be done, on earth as it is in heaven. Give us this day our daily bread. And forgive us our trespasses, against us. And lead us not into temptation but deliver us from evil. For thine is the kingdom, and the power, and the glory, forever and ever Amen." Walter knew what he had done was wrong, not only to Lola, but to Peaches too. He did the same thing to her. He used to wait until Peaches was asleep when she was younger before going into her bedroom and play away in her panties. "Preying on innocent little girls that's how you get off? You fuckin' creep!" She exclaimed. Walter than mumbled, "I'm sorry! " Although he had one hand cuffed, he was able to grab the gun from Peaches. He closed his eyes and told her he was sorry. The next thing she heard, "POW!" There, on her kitchen floor lay Walters body, limp and lifeless. She couldn't believe it. This nigga really took the coward's way out and killed himself. She hysterically dialed 9-1-1, "9-1-1, What's Your Emergency?" "Yes, I need to report a suicide," she told the operator. By the time paramedics arrived, Leah, Annie, and Eazy were already there. No one could believe what happened. Leah didn't want to believe what happened. She hadn't seen her father in years, but when she finally does, she finds out he's a pedophile and then killed himself, it was just too much to comprehend. That bastard could burn in the pits of hell for all Peaches cared. "Motherfucker had the nerve. He must not have known who he was fuckin' wit," Peaches thought. Although they were no longer dating or engaged, Eazy still stood by her. He came to support her and see what was going on, but all she could think was, "How dare you?" as she looked at her father's dead body. She was numb to the bullshit. She was interrupted in her thoughts by hearing a phone ring, "Whose phone keeps ringing?" Then she noticed that it was Walter's phone, it must've fallen out of his pocket while they were tussling. Peaches picked it up and saw he had 13 missed calls and 100 text messages, so she went through them all. She couldn't believe what she was reading. He kept calling and calling and calling. So, finally, she answered, "Hello!" The voice on the other end replied, "Yes, hi, is Walter around? Peaches answered and said, "No, he is not. He left his phone." "May I ask who I'm speaking too?" he asked. She quickly said, "Peaches! I'm his daughter, who is this"? "I'm Bruce, his lover," he responded with no hesitation. She put the phone on speaker and asked if he could repeat himself, so everyone could hear, "I said I'm Bruce, your father's lover. What happened?" Annie began to cry heavily, she couldn't believe that she actually laid down with and had kids with this monster, not only one, but two. Everyone was in total shock. Annie hadn't seen the signs, but they were there. Seems like they both had something in common; Peaches and Annie both sucked when it came to finding a good man. Walter and Annie's relationship was just like Peaches and Eazy's, but it was the money and the cars that Annie was attracted too. This situation had Peaches thinking how Annie didn't know this was going on? Those nights he snuck out of bed to go get off on his child and not the woman he married was sickening. Annie was now sitting on the sofa, Peaches walked over and sat beside her and grabbed her mother's hand and held it tight. She looked in Annie's eyes and said, "When I was a child, Walter used to molest me." "Why are you just now saying something, Peaches?" Annie asked? Peaches replied, "I didn't know then what I know now. I wasn't aware what was being done to me until I saw him standing over my baby. I remember going in and out of my sleep as a child at night and would see him standing beside my bed. He took advantage of me while I was asleep. And he did the same thing to my child." Peaches thanked God that Lola was asleep because she knew some kids get molested knowing who the perverts were. She then began to tell her mother that she would not be attending his funeral and didn't want to discuss him or the situation ever again. Annie told Peaches that she understood and that she was so sorry for not being there to protect her as a child; they held each other, and both cried like babies. Leah really didn't know what to think, she was team "Walter" and Peaches couldn't understand why.

It's was now 4:00am, everyone was exhausted; it had been a crazy night. Peaches didn't want to live in this house anymore and all she could think of was moving; staying in that house gave her the creeps. Eazy asked if she wanted him to stay but Peaches didn't answer, she was too busy in her thoughts. They all feel asleep on the couch and Eazy camped out on the floor, not too far from where Peaches laid. He loved her dearly and continued to be consistent when it came to getting his woman back, but little did he know, Eazy was in for a rude awakening.

Chapter 7

"Incredible"

When Lola rolled over, Peaches was lying right beside her, watching her sleep. "Hey, Princess!" she said before planting a kiss on her cheek. "Hi, Mommy!" she said. "Lola, do you remember what happened last night?" Peaches asked. Lola looked at Peaches like she was confused at the question. She responded, "Yeah, Santa Claus came!" Peaches laughed. Peaches got Lola dressed because she needed to go get her checked out to see if Walter harmed her in any way. Once they arrived, she was admitted because they wanted to check her out thoroughly. They did notice Lola was swollen a little in her vagina area. Peaches began to cry at the fact the man that she called "dad" was a monster in disguise. She held Lola and began to apologize for not being there to protect her. Peaches' phone rang,

"Hello!" It was Eazy, "You ok?" he asked. "I'm headed, home I'll call you later," she said. "But, no, Baby, I wanna talk to you now! Are you ok?" Eazy replied, "I know it's hard for you, I just wanna let you know I'm here."

Once she got home, the doorbell rang, "Coming," she shouted. It was Leah, but before she could even get in the house good, Leah asked what kind of funeral arrangements she wanted to make for Walter? Peaches was infuriated just hearing that man's name. "I'm not attending his funeral, nor am I making plans," she replied, "didn't you hear me tell mom that?" "Just let it go, Peaches," Leah replied. "Let what go?" Peaches asked. "Just let God handle it," was Leah's response. "What if the shoe was on the other foot?" Peaches asked, "Do you think it would be that easy to just let it go?" "Well, you need some time to think to yourself. I'll take my niece for a while. "Yay!" Lola loved the sound of that. "You not going to work today?" Leah asked. Peaches responded, "Nope! I have some errands I need to handle." Once Leah and Lola left, Peaches got dressed and headed to the nearest bar. Her hair was tied back, she wore a pair of high top Italian Pucc Leovono sneakers, a pair of Pucc Leovono stretch pants with a Pucc Leovono halter to match, and her gold Rolex which was blinging as always. She was simple and cute, nothing major. While cruising around, Peaches decided to stop by the nearest florist shop. Zay had been on her mind for a while so she was going to go to the cemetery. Once she arrived, she couldn't remember where Zay was. It took her about 10 mins before she could find him. "Zay, where are you?" she asked? Her keys fell to the ground and while bending down, guess who was right there? Zay. Peaches smiled, she knew it was him saying, "I'm right here." She sat, talked, and cried for about an hour or two. As she headed back to her car, she thought a nice cocktail would do her good right about now, so she headed over to Atlantic Grill. As Peaches strutted in the bar, she sat and ordered two shots of Disaronno. Then, out of nowhere, this guy sat right beside her ordered her another round. She looked up and was speechless. This nigga was handsome, well-groomed, smelled good, and was looking like a bag of money. "Hi! My name is Rashad," as he extended his hand out to shake hers. "My name is Peaches. It's nice to meet you," she said as she tossed her shots back. He smiled and stated, "Sweet name like you, huh!? So, tell me something good, Miss. Peaches." She rolled her eyes and shook her head. The drinks were kicking in, she just wanted to enjoy the moment. it was like a rush that made everything that hurt, feel so good.

He saw Peaches wasn't really in a talkative mood, so he ordered more drinks. He said, "Well, I'll start it off." She stopped him and said, "Look, what's up? What is it that you want from me? Everybody I've ever loved has hurt me to the core," she shook her head and remained silent. Rashad didn't respond, he just listened. He began to speak again, "I'm here for a business meeting across the street at the Atlantic Station and decided to come over and have a drink to celebrate." Peaches asked, "Celebrate for what?" He continued, "I'm from B'more but I reside in Dubai. I'm a fashion designer and just signed my first contract deal with *Chanel*. I'm loving your outfit by the way." "Thanks!" she replied. He was different, but in a good way. But Peaches wasn't ready for anybody no time soon. She was a flawed and broken individual on the inside. It's crazy how fucked up other people's actions can turn you into a monster. Rashad could've sat and chatted with Peaches all day, her beauty had him caught in her web. His cockiness turned her on. Hell, the man's presence alone was dangerous. His mouth piece was vicious, something had come over Peaches just by his conversation, it felt like magic. It seemed as though he knew what to say and how to say it. He was a very intelligent young man and everything about him, that she knew so far, was incredible.

Chapter 8

"Wacko"

Two months had gone by and Peaches was settling in her new home. Every morning she received a dozen roses from the *Glamour's Collection,* different colors every day. The chemistry between those two was just in sync, a day didn't go by without them talking, texting or facetime. There was something about this man that Peaches couldn't put her finger on, Rashad was different than any man she ever dated. Making sure Peaches and Lola were ok was his first priority. They only knew each other for about three months but it felt more like three years. Peaches could talk to Rashad about anything, no matter what the situation was or how busy he could've been, being there for Peaches was not a problem. Late nights on the phone made her feel like her old high school days all over again. When

Peaches was tired from having a long day and having to take care of Lola, she would fall asleep on the phone. Rashad didn't mind, he thought it was cute, as along as he knew she was home and safe. She always tried her hardest to stay up, that's how bad she loved this man's conversation. It was 2:00am, Peaches line beeped, it was Eazy. She didn't even bother to answer but he continued calling back to back. It didn't bother her one bit, she just ignored his ass. She was a good woman to Eazy, and now that he fucked up, he couldn't handle it. "So, when is our next date?" he asked. Peaches began blushing and responded, "Whenever you're." After that night, Rashad flew back and forth from Dubai to Atlanta often to see this woman that he adored. Eazy had a feeling something was different, Peaches was more distant. He was so blind, he couldn't see that Peaches was gone and no longer had any feelings for him. He didn't know it, but it was over for him, there was a knew sheriff in town. The very next day, Friday night, Peaches dropped Lola off at her mom's house because it was Rell's weekend to have her. So, she chilled there for about an hour before leaving. She gave Lola a kiss and told her mom she'd call her later. When she got into her car, shock and fear overpowered her; she wasn't in the car alone. There was a man in her car. She didn't know who it could be as his face was covered and he was wearing all black. He told her to drive and gave directions on where to go, all the while holding a gun up to her head. She was filled with terror and didn't know what to think. He saw Peaches was terrified and he loved it. He told her if she made any false moves, she was dead, and he meant every word. Her phone began to ring and tears began to fall down her face. She wanted to answer so bad. "I dare you!" he replied. She knew what that meant so she continued driving to the destination and prayed the whole way there. They pulled up to an abandoned building, and he immediately covered her eyes. "Please don't kill me!" Peaches cried. "CLAP" He hit her across the face so hard she fell to the ground. "Don't Say A Word!" he yelled as he yanked Peaches by her hair.

His voice sounded familiar, but the wacko didn't talk much. Holding her closely to him, he escorted her to the abandoned building. Once inside, she was thrown to the ground. Peaches groaned as she scooted to the wall for security. "Where you going?" he laughed while aggressively pulling her pants off. She began to kick and scream and since her hands were free, she swung and tried to pull his ears off. "I'm taking this pussy, it was mine first to begin with." She screamed, "Chill the fuck out!" He didn't like that and punched her in the head, "Whack!" He hit her so hard she blacked out. Rell fucked her until she bled. "You brought this on yourself. That Nigga got you smelling yourself, got you thinking you the shit now, huh?" Both her eyes were black and blue, her lip was busted, and her body was limp and sore. Once Peaches realized it was Rell's voice she was hearing, she knew she was dead. She was all cried out, so she began praying. She knew this was her karma from Tori. The room was empty, smelly, and mold was everywhere. The floor was wet, and bugs were crawling on Peaches, she couldn't move. Every time she tried to move, Rell would punish her. He stood with a belt in his hand and told her, "I'mma beat yo ass like your daddy should of did." Not knowing what happened between his daughter and Walter. Peaches was furious, she wanted the man she was once head over hills for as a teenager dead. "You gonna take me away from our baby?" she whispered? Arguing or fighting with this man wasn't gonna help Peaches. She realized Rell had lost his mind. He didn't answer. Peaches saw his face, he looked possessed and evil was all over him. She started crying again. "Don't start that cry baby shit, Bitch! I'm not going for that. Remember you hit me, Bitch, in my head with a pistol? You forgot about that, huh? And got me locked up. I told you, yo ass was mine, didn't I?" as he kicked Peaches to show her how serious he was. "Please!" she cried. "Shut up, Bitch! I'm showing you no mercy. You gonna meet your maker today." Rell tortured Peaches for three days. Annie was trying to reach Peaches because Rell never showed up. Rashad and Peaches had plans that day, he knew something wasn't right. Rashad had been calling for three days and got no answer or return phone call. He was flying home to see what was going home. When he arrived at the airport, he began to scratch his head going back and forth as to whether or not he should really fly back to the US. He hadn't met any of her family, other than Lola, so he didn't have anyone to call. What was he going to do when he arrived and she wasn't home? Eazy, on the other hand, knew something was wrong. When Rashad arrived at Peaches' house that day, he waited and waited and called her phone nonstop and began to think for sure something was wrong. As he stepped out of his white on white 2018 Land Rover Sport to leave a message in Peaches' mailbox, a car pulled up. He stepped back to the car and pulled out his pistol. He noticed it was an older woman, so he relaxed and put his pistol away. It was Annie, she was also looking for Peaches. She rolled her window down to ask him who he was and what he was doing in her daughter's yard. After finding out who Rashad was,

Annie told him that Peaches was missing, and everyone has been looking for her. Knowing Peaches was missing made him sick to his stomach. He told Annie to file a missing person's report. After this chance meeting, Rashad kept in contact with Annie. Meanwhile, Peaches lay helpless. With her heartbeat beginning to slow down, she knew she was dying. She was dying, and this bastard left her for dead. She knew there was no hope for her. Peaches felt a cold breeze enter the room but she couldn't open her eyes. The presence she felt was uneasy, it stood over her and whispered in her ear, "YOU GOT ME KILLED!" Peaches knew right away it was Tori. "Wake up!" she told herself. Then she began to pray, "God, I'm sorry. Please forgive me, I have a daughter to raise. Please don't take me now." There she laid, numb, and cold. Peaches died. A bright light appeared, and she heard an unfamiliar noise beeeepppppppp... Then she felt her spirit leave her body. She reached the light and stood next to a beautiful white horse. It was so real. It stood there wagging its long thick mane and she couldn't believe what she was seeing. "Wake up! Wake up!" is what she kept telling herself. A familiar face appeared, he was handsome, wearing all white. He began walking towards her, when he got closer, she saw it was Zay. He hugged her and as she tried to speak, she couldn't. He told her he had to go. "Nooooo!" she cried, "Please don't leave me again!" within a blink of an eye he was gone. Peaches than heard an irritating voice, "Good morning! Good morning! Rise and shine sleepy head." She tried to open her eyes but couldn't. She felt better than before, the atmosphere seemed different. She felt warm, she wasn't cold anymore. "Where am I?" she asked, with tears rolling down her face. The voice of a woman said, "Aww, don't cry sweetie, you are safe here. Can you hear me? Nod your head for, Yes." Peaches nodded and tried to speak. The calm voice then told her, "Just get you some rest. You're at North Georgia Hospital, you were admitted here 3 weeks ago. We need you to get well so we can locate your family. Her eyes remained shut, "Thank you, God! I'm alive!" Peaches wanted to go ballistic, but she did what she was told and remained calm; she needed all of her strength for what was about to go down.

A week later, Peaches woke up to a kiss on her forehead from Rashad - she jumped out of fear. Being startled forced her to speak, but her throat was sore. She then noticed Eazy standing on the opposite side of the hospital bed. He handed Peaches a cup of water to drink. She was only able to sip a little because it hurt to swallow. Eazy was ready for Peaches to recover, he was eager to find out what Nigga did this to her. Rashad knew exactly who Eazy was; Peaches was up front from the start. She signaled for a pen. "She's trying to tell us something," Rashad said. Peaches wrote the letter R with her hand, she was trying to do sign language. Eazy shouted, "Rell!" She shook her head in terror and she began crying and shaking. "I knew it!" Eazy replied, he left the room without saying a word. Two hours later, Eazy returned with Annie and Lola. Peaches was crying with tears of joy and her baby started when she saw her mom. It had been almost a month since Lola saw her mom, they have never been apart more than a day or two. Annie kissed Peaches and then Leah walked through the door, happy that her sister was still alive. Rashad was still at Peaches' beside. Whoever thought he was going somewhere had another thing coming, the bond they created was stronger than her and Eazy's had ever been. Every time Peaches heard a knock at the door, Eazy and Rashad noticed the fear that engulfed her. Rashad made it his mission to find this Nigga. The two of them never said a word to each other while in the hospital room. Before the doctor discharged Peaches, Eazy asked if she would come stay with him until she got better. Rashad stepped out of the room to take a phone call. Eazy told Peaches, "I don't know who this Nigga is, but I'm not leaving you or Lola with him. I don't care how long you been fucking him." On the other hand, Rashad was making arrangements for Peaches and Lola to fly back home with him. She then whispered to Eazy, "I'm grown! I make my own decisions." If looks could kill, she would've been dead two times. Eazy was so pissed he wanted to destroy everything in the hospital room. But instead, he stepped outside and told Rashad the plans he arranged for Peaches. Rashad was still on a call while Eazy was talking to him. Rashad covered the phone receiver with his hand and politely told Eazy to get the fuck out his face! Rashad didn't like the fact that Eazy was trying to control the situation; knowing damn well Peaches didn't even want his ass. Once Rashad ended the call all hell broke loose. Rashad and Eazy began arguing back and forth, and loudly, at that. Annie had to rush out to break it up and she told Eazy to leave so he could cool off. "Naw, Mommy, why this bitch ass Nigga can't leave?" "Bitch ass Nigga?" Rashad repeated. "Aye, my Nigga, you better do what's right and go cool off like she said," Rashad shouted back. Before they knew it, Peaches was out of bed and at the door trying to see what was going on. When Rashad saw her, he panicked, "Aww, Babe, you're not supposed to be up." He helped Peaches back to bed. Before

Eazy could leave, she called him back into the room. Whispering, to them both, "Look, this is to the both of you, I can't take this arguing. What y'all need to be doing is going out and find the Nigga who did this to me." Eazy shot back, "It's already done!" with an asshole grin on his face. No matter how bad Eazy fucked up, Peaches belonged to him, he didn't care what nobody had to say, not even her. Rashad was unbothered by Eazy's Superman antics, he was an asshole. Annie and Leah decided to leave to get washed up and grab a bite to eat. "I don't think you need to leave me here with these two, Momma," Peaches whispered to Annie.

The both of them were stuck to Peaches like glue. Eazy looked at Rashad and said, "I ain't going nowhere, Nigga!" "I ain't neither, Nigga!" Rashad replied back. Peaches shook her head and told Eazy to go home and get some rest, she was ok. "So, you choosing him over me?" he shouted. "Eazy, just leave!" Peaches replied. He swung the door so hard that it almost came off the hinges. Everyone left but

Rashad. "You ok?" he asked. "I'm ok," Peaches replied. Holding her hand, Rashad said, "It's on you Peaches, what do you wanna do?" "Well, I wanna go home to pack my things and move. I don't trust Rell. Eazy said he handled it, but I'm not sure what's going on. I need to protect my baby from her crazy ass daddy," she told him. Then about 8:30pm there was a knock at the door. Rashad walked to the door and opened it without asking who it was. "Hi! I'm officer Scott from the Atlanta police department. I'm here to ask a few questions about what happened three weeks ago?" Rashad asked Peaches if she felt like talking, she told the officer she didn't remember anything. She didn't see his face, but she did remember where she left her car. Peaches gave the officer the information, he thanked her for her time and told Peaches she would be hearing from him soon. The very next day, Rashad had some movers go to Peaches' house and pack up everything and put it in storage. This gave Peaches time to decide where she wanted to move. Rashad helped Peaches into his truck and once she was buckled in, she realized she didn't have a phone. She needed to check her emails for work. Rashad stopped at AT&T and bought her a new phone; she had to keep the same number because she had no contacts.

Peaches then made the decision for her and Lola to move to Dubai to be with Rashad. He always made her feel safe. 8 months had gone by and Peaches saw how beautiful Dubai was and didn't want to ever return back home; she was happy to be away from Georgia. Not wanting to be in the way or be a distraction to Rashad, she decided to rent a condo for about a year just to relax and get her thoughts together. Eazy was furious with her decision. He told Peaches to tell Rashad, "If anything happens to you, he's dead." He couldn't stand the situation, but he had to respect it. He called her every day and would tell her, "I love you! I thought we were even? Enough is enough come back home." For Peaches, it wasn't that easy, she had never been out of Georgia her whole life. She was happy with the decision she made, not just for herself, but for Lola, too. Peaches was lying in bed, she had the perfect view, right across from the Burj Al Arab Hotel. If she could lay there for forever, she would. Her phone rang, it was Annie, "Hey, Ma! How's everything?" She told Peaches everything was fine and that they found Rell's body near the Chattahoochee River. Peaches didn't respond. "Did you receive the postcard I sent?" she asked Annie. "Yes, Baby, I've got it," she replied. Peaches told Annie she was going to send for her and Leah to send her some dates that would fit everyone's schedules. They both said their goodbyes and ended the call.

Even though Rashad had his own home and bed, he stayed at Peaches most of the time. She couldn't get rid of this guy. The connection they had was amazing, they were both Gemini's and very compatible. She hadn't heard from Eazy, she was hoping he got the point and moved on, knowing he's the reason why they were not together. Before getting out of bed, Peaches began to recite. Psalm

91. Everything was beginning to take a toll on her, "Regardless of what I've been through, I have to keep going," she told herself. While Lola was still sleeping, Peaches decided to shower. Her bathroom was to die for, she had two of everything and a TV; Rashad made sure she was lived lavishly. Her wardrobe was out of this world. One day, Peaches came home from the grocery store and Rashad surprised her with furniture from Benetti's Italia Furniture. Lola was even draped in Pucc Leovono attire. Both Lola's and Peaches' closets were full. Peaches had every color fur, let's not forget the jewelry; she was iced out. Before getting out of the tub, Rashad was standing there, waiting, patiently for Peaches to finish. He loved how Peaches looked, it was different from all the other women he had been with. Peaches was the trophy type. Even though Rashad had options, and females were always flocking at his feet, he wasn't interested. Peaches, on the other hand, hadn't gave him any pussy yet and that made him love her even more. It was something about her that nobody else had. One

thing for sure, two things for certain, he was going to find out. "Hey, Sweetie!" he greeted her with a kiss on the forehead. Rashad was always clean, just looking at this man turned Peaches on, he was wearing a tailored Armani suit that fit his figure just right. Peaches could've nutted on herself by just looking at him. His hair was thick and long down his back. Rashad was mixed with Cherokee and Black, he had never been married and had no kids, except for Lola, who he adored. Eazy missed Peaches like crazy, he'd call just to talk to her. Peaches knew Eazy was hurting, but she was too getting away for a while, it was what she needed and deep down inside, Eazy knew it too. He just couldn't stomach the fact that this new Nigga was about to take his place.

Rashad was helping Peaches get dressed, "I've made plans for all of us today. I got somethings I wanna go over with you." he stated. Peaches wore a long white fitted Giorgio Armani dress with a pair of Armani slippers that showed her manicured toes and her coke bottle shape. While Peaches tied her hair back, Rashad watched; she was also half Cherokee and her shape was out of this world. They loved looking at each other. When she would catch him looking, she'd just blush, and he would do the same.

Once she got Lola dressed, they went out to enjoy the beautiful day. Rashad planned a nice lunch at Phi Thai. Peaches had never experienced this type of lifestyle, at the restaurant they sat outside on the terrace to take in the scenery. The view was across the Madinat's tranquil waterways. While eating, Rashad asked Peaches, "How do you like living here? Could you make this your home for good?" Peaches replied, "I love it here! I would want to send for my mom and sister though, I miss them a lot." Rashad told Peaches to think about it and maybe they could work something out. His phone began to ring. "Yo!" he answered, the person on the other end was loud. Peaches rolled her eyes, it sounded like the bitch was ratchet. Rashad didn't even respond to the call he just hung up. "Your wife?" Peaches asked sarcastically. He smiled, "Hell no! She's just a chick I fuck from time to time." "Oh, ok!" Peaches responded while nodding her head. "Anything serious that I need to know about?" She replied. "Naw, nothing serious, Babe," he assured her. Then Peaches' phone began to ring, it was Eazy, she didn't answer. "So, this Nigga really love you huh?" Rashad asked. "Why you say that?" she continued, "You don't hurt people you love," with a stank face. "Well, even though he fucked up, he's still trying to show you he loves you," Rashad told Peaches. "But guess what? HIS LOSS!!" Rashad shouted out loud and Peaches laughed. "So, what did he do to you?" Rashad asked. "He cheated on me with a piece of shit." Peaches eyes rolled so far behind her head it was ridiculous, "He introduced that hoe as his sister. I would've never thought he would stoop that low." Peaches was still in shock just by talking about it. How could he go from sugar to shit, she thought to herself? Rashad shook his head as he listened. He turned his head to get a glimpse of the scenery, he rested his hand under his chin and began to rub his beard. Rashad then said to Peaches, "Dogs attract bitches, kings attract queens. You're not the right woman for that Nigga. He gives me bum vibes, you must've been desperate to fuck with that Nigga?" He said, with a straight face. Peaches almost coked off her champagne and flicked Rashad the finger. Lola was occupied on her tablet. Normally, no one exists to her when she's on that thing. Peaches sometimes has to take it from her and today was one of those days, "Mommy be wanting some attention from you," she told Lola while planting a kiss on her cheek. "You ok, Bookie?" That was her nickname "I'm ok, Mommy. I'm just chillin'" she responded as Rashad laughed. "I wanted to talk to you about becoming my assistant Peaches." Rashad blurted out. "Your assistant?" she asked, shocked and hesitant at the same time. "Yes! You have the mindset of a business woman and you're already an entrepreneur. I think it would be a great fit for you." Peaches told Rashad she needed some time to think about it. "No need to rush, I want you to take your time. Relax, don't worry about anything. I want you to enjoy your new life," he told her. She looked at him with a smile and they both raised their glasses in the air and gave a toast to the good life. "Cheers!"

Chapter 9

"Til Death Do Us Part"

A year later, Peaches was living her best life with Rashad and his business was expanding daily. Arabic language is what they both insisted on learning. Even Lola wanted to learn, and she was only five. This was a power couple in the making, ready to take over the world. Today was a big day for Rashad, one of the biggest fashion shows was showcasing at the most fashionable hotel. The three-day fashion event was about luxury and fashion, beauty and lifestyle. The runway shows and trade shows were featuring international brands and works by some of the region's biggest designers along with cultures from Africa, China, and Italy. Peaches made sure Rashad's models were prepared: hair, make up etc. When it came to being his assistant, she was getting the hang of it and doing her thang. His models were from different cultures and came in many different sizes and flavas. While helping the models get ready for the big show, Peaches received a text from Annie, who was now living in Dubai along with her sister, Leah. Leah was interested in working with Peaches and Rashad, she was into fashion also. Peaches hired a teacher to home school Leah and told her to finish school and to choose any college. Leah wanted to become a pediatrician, but from what she was seeing, fashion was where the money was. Once Leah graduated she would take a class for design/fashion. All she and Annie did was shop, they got lost almost every time they left the house. Dubai was different, and they were trying to learn their way around. Peaches texted them how to get back home. She bought Annie her dream house so that she would be comfortable. Peaches wasn't planning on moving anytime soon and wanted everyone close. Everything went as planned and the show was successful. There were so many designers that attended, from Louis Vuitton to Chanel to Tom Ford and Giorgio Armani, etc.

It was time for Rashad to take his catwalk with his models. Peaches wasn't aware that Rashad wanted her to walk with him and they were wearing matching Chanel outfits from head to toe. Peaches was as fly as he was. They lit up everywhere they went. A glow appeared when they were together and it showed. Peaches was proud of her man; he was smart, intelligent, had dignity, and spoke with confidence. He hugged Peaches, "We did it!" is what he whispered in her ear. While exiting the stage, a fashion designer by the name of Abdu, from Nigeria, was pleased to meet Rashad and wanted to introduce him to his daughter Ada. Abdu was about to hand his empire over to his only daughter. She was beautiful. She shook Rashad's hand, and, not once, did she acknowledge Peaches. "My daughter wanted to know if you were available later for dinner?" he asked. "Sure, my fiancé and I would be happy to attend." Rashad responded. Ada gave

Peaches a nasty look but kept her cool. She wanted Rashad bad and wasn't about to let anyone interfere with what she had up her sleeve. Ada was the Queen of Nigeria, she was a spoiled bitch that got everything she wanted. Her mission was to find a king to take back home to Africa. Ada was in for a rude awakening. It would only be over Peaches' dead body that the likes of Ada would capture Rashad's heart. Ada was gonna have to kill Peaches for Rashad. Now that Rashad referenced Peaches as his fiancé, she was on cloud nine. Rashad didn't know it yet, but Peaches was gonna be the perfect wife that he could ever ask for. Peaches noticed the shade that was thrown but stood confidently next to her man. "Bitch, please!" Peaches thought, while looking at the musty tramp; you could smell her from where she stood. Ada smelled like a whooper with extra onions. Don't get me wrong, Ada was beautiful and had plenty money as her family was truly wealthy. Her father was getting up in age and passing his empire down to his baby was an honor. The reason she was single is because Ada had a bird brain. The bitch was dumb as a door knob. Peaches noticed Ada couldn't keep her eyes off of her man while they stood there chatting. Peaches kissed Rashad on his cheek and asked if she could be excused. Peaches wasn't insecure, she was a woman with confidence and very comfortable in her own skin. She couldn't stand next to that slut any longer and she knew Rashad wasn't going anywhere. She just wished stankin' Ada knew it as well. About twenty minutes later Rashad headed to the back where he found Peaches. He was holding a meeting to thank everyone for coming. To show his appreciation, he was hosting an after party at the Cirque Le Soir Night Club; this was going to be an epic event. Knowing this was Rashad's party, Ada made sure her grand entrance would catch Rashad's attention because everything Ada wanted Ada got. After the show, Rashad and Peaches decided to have a drink at the bar and have a toast. They sat so close to each other they could smell each other's breath. Their lips touched, his kisses were soft and gentle. Peaches didn't want him to stop. They held hands as they sat and talked. "You did a very good job today," he told Peaches as he planted a kiss on her neck. She smiled, "Thank you, Babe! I couldn't have done it without you." After arriving home, Rashad walked Peaches to her door (they lived in the same building). He told Peaches to call him once she got dressed and she blew him a kiss before closing the door. Before she jumped in the shower, she shot Rashad a text, "What are we wearing?" He said, "I'll get dressed first and then we go from there." "Ok!" she smiled as she hung up the phone. Before running her bath water, Peaches went to the fridge, she was craving some spinach dip and chips. While soaking her body she rolled a joint to ease her mind and with every puff she became more relaxed. Her phone rang, it was Eazy. Peaches was beginning to feel sorry for his ass so she answered, "Hello!" "Everything good? You ok?" he asked. "We're ok. How about you?" she asked. Eazy replied, "I miss my family. I'll do whatever to piece us back together. I'm sorry for everything I've done. I need you to know I'm a changed man." The phone remained silent, "You still there?" he asked? "Yeah, I'm here." Peaches replied, she continued by telling Eazy, "What we had wasn't real. You loved me, but you also took me for granted. I wasted time I can never get back." Furiously he said, "I made you look good." Peaches snapped, "How dare you! Do you not know who I am? I only gave you a chance, Nigga, because I was vulnerable at the time. You betrayed me. I showed you my loyalty. Just imagine, I could be lying next to you right now. You fucked that up, not me!" Eazy didn't interrupt, he held the phone and listened, then said, "You mines! I had you first! You're my bitch." "Bitch!" Peaches interrupted, "if anybody's a bitch, it's you! Eazy, you stay on my line, what is it that you want from me? You've received your ring." "Peaches, you don't know nothing about this man," Eazy replied. She cut him off, "Ain't that the pot calling the kettle black. I thought I knew you, but from the looks of it, you just like any ole regular Nigga. I should've never gave you the benefit of the doubt. Look, I have to go,

I've already wasted too much time on this phone with you." Eazy wasn't taking no for an answer and said, "That night I was about to marry you, Peaches. 'Til death do us part." "We're not married, Eazy." He told Peaches, "Imma ask you nicely to come back home, this will be my last time." "CLICK!" Peaches hung up. "Dumb fuck," she muttered. "You call me names too after we hang up?" she didn't notice Rashad was standing there all along. "Creep!" Peaches shouted. "Looking good babe!" Rashad wore all white Pucc Leovono attire: a Pucc shirt, Pucc joggers with a fresh pair of high top, Italy cup suede, red and green sneakers. He sported a white, green, and red scarf around his head as a headband that read: Pucc Leovono. He wore an aqua marine pinky ring; His watch alone was worth 200k. He knew his woman was about to kill it; Peaches wore her matching black lace Victoria secret bra and panty set. A green red and white Pucc Leovono mini dress that had spaghetti straps, with the low top green and red Italian cup sneakers. She pressed her hair which made it flow down her back looking like a thick silky mane. Her makeup was just right. Her jewelry was also drippin' the earrings Rashad bought her were worth 200k. There Rolex's were his and hers. While getting dressed, she was receiving a face time call, it was Lola. "Hey, Momma!" "Hey, Bookie!" Peaches responded, "I'm about to make some cookies for Nana." "Ok! Save me some." Peaches responded. Lola told Peaches, "Momma, you look so pretty." Annie was in the background, "You look nice, Peaches. You know you get that beauty from your Momma, right?" Annie asked. Peaches laughed, Yeah, I know beauty runs in the family. I'll call y'all later. Mom, thanks for watching Lola for me, Love you guys!"

They pulled up to the party in a 2018 Mercedes Maybach S600 all white leather interior. It was a red-carpet event. As they were about to step on the scene, Ada was right next to them being carried in by two white stallions. Ada wore all gold: a two-piece lace chiffon maxi long dress. Big gold anklets on both legs with no shoes. Her hair was braided into a ponytail that came down to her ass. As soon as they walked through the day, pictures were being snapped, with famous bloggers, photographers, and designers trying to get to know Rashad. He was a 37-year-old black man from Baltimore that came from nothing. Fashion was his passion and he was fulfilling his dream. His style was crazy stupid. When it came to designing, the man really used his imagination and his brand was expanding all over the world. He was even invited to appear on Oprah. Peaches was having a good time until made her presence known by giving them both a hug. She shocked the shit out of Peaches! "She's not musty tonight," Peaches giggled to herself. She wanted to make sure Rashad got a swift of the Bald'afrique she was wearing. "May I have this dance?" she asked Peaches. Peaches knew Ada was no competition, so she told her, "Sure, why not?" *Top Off* by Jay Z was blasting loud through the speakers, Peaches noticed Ada had some nice moves, but she was about to give her a run for her money. It seemed as though they were having a dance battle. Peaches finished by giving Rashad a nice little lap dance. Ada didn't mind, she began to give Peaches a lap dance. By this time, everyone was really enjoying themselves, Rashad and Ada had Peaches in a sandwich. Ace of Spade bottles were being popped left and right; they had the biggest hookahs in their VIP section. Peaches was grinding all on her man. Rashad was on cloud nine and he was proud of himself. He felt good knowing his dreams were being accomplished and he was finally living his best life. This was a celebration to remember. Peaches told Rashad she needed to go freshen up he said, "I'll take you, My Love." He was so loving, warm, and compassionate. Peaches loved every bit of him. As they walked, magic was happening, they were both glowing. Where they went, it seemed like Ada went also. Peaches would look back and see Ada smiling to herself. "You can't compete where you don't compare," Peaches told Ada.

Ada shot Peaches a birdie. It was funny knowing Ada wanted something she couldn't have. "I'll be right here when you come out," he told Peaches. As Rashad waited, a blogger walked up from behind and tapped his shoulder, when he turned around, he noticed this sexy, chocolate of woman standing in front of him. He sized her up really quickly and thought she was a foreigner because of her exotic looks. "Hi! I blog for *Sippinlemondae*, can I get a picture?" Mesmerized by her beauty, he slowly said, "Sure!" and quickly cleared his throat. Her beauty simply radiated, she had aqua dreads which were shoulder length and she was thick in all the right places. She was a stallion. As Peaches open the bathroom stall, she heard, "'til death do us part." She was face-to-face with Eazy, POW! POW!... to be continued

Acknowledgement's

First and foremost I would like to give all praises to God my Lord, and Savior without Him nothing is possible. I want to acknowledge and give thanks to Dr. Nichol Burris, Parice C. Parker, Pucc Leovono along with my beautiful family. May God continues to bless you all.

P.S. Chi thank you for giving birth to me, and you are the real MVP!

Shior la queen

Contact the Author

Shior la queen

instagram@FlawedTheBook

Fountain of Life Publishers House

P. O. Box 922612, Norcross, GA 30010

Phone: 404.936.3989

For book orders or wholesale distribution

Website: www.pariceparker.biz

Made in the USA
Lexington, KY
15 December 2019